BOOK 4

TOBY ANDREWS AND THE JUNIOR DEPUTIES

NEIGHBORHOOD'S SCARIEST WOMAN

BOOK 4

TOBY ANDREWS AND THE JUNIOR DEPUTIES

THE
NEIGHBORHOOD'S SCARIEST WOMAN

JERRY B. JENKINS
Author of The Dallas O'Neill Mystery Series

MOODY PRESS
CHICAGO

JL
J417 n

ISBN: 0-8024-1628-4

1 3 5 7 9 10 8 6 4 2

Printed in the United States of America

To childhood friends

Contents

The Mysterious Mrs. Butchbaker

Normally I hate the last week of summer before school starts. But this year was the greatest. With my little sister Kate off at Grandma's, Mom and Dad said I could have the other junior deputies—all four of them—over for the whole week. We had plenty of room, and if we promised to keep the noise down—especially at night—we could do it.

It was great, because during the school year we see each other only at church, except Thomas Christian and I, of course. Old Tom and I go to the same school and are in the same grade, but we are in different classrooms.

I call him Old Tom because, though he's our age, he looks so much older than the rest of us. He looks old enough to drive. He's tall and dark with curly black hair and has muscles and sharp, defined features. He lives at the Lake Farm Home, and he's afraid of nothing and no one. He's usually quiet, except when it's just Tom and I. For some reason he likes and trusts me, so he can talk to me about anything.

I'm captain of the junior deputies, and he's lieutenant. At church Sunday he wanted to make sure everybody was packed and ready to come. The plan was that they would ride home with my parents and me and then would be delivered back next Sunday after church.

Big Tom and I always refer to the other three by their nicknames. Jonathan Bynum we call Red Jon because of his red hair. Daniel Jackson, a huge black kid, we call Big Dan for obvious reasons. And the small and skinny Joel McBride, two years younger than the rest of us, is known as Little Joel.

I admit I was glad Kate would be away for the week. She's all right for a little sister, but she naturally wants to be in on every case the junior deputies take, and often that just doesn't work. Then she gets cranky and is no fun to live with.

Three of the guys were glad she would be gone too, I think, but they wouldn't admit it. Little Joel was probably disappointed she was gone, but he for sure wouldn't admit *that*. He was always saying he didn't like Kate and Kate didn't like him, but we all knew the truth. He was only two years older than she was, and they kind of looked alike, both with blond hair and really cute.

Old Tom urged me to round up the guys between Sunday school and church and make sure nobody had to go home first and get something he forgot. "It's just like you guys to waste the first afternoon going back for your toothbrush or your teddy bear!" he said.

That made Red Jon laugh and shake his head, causing that hair to shoot out sideways and make him look like a clown. "Your toothbrush or your teddy bear!" he repeated, cackling. He grew suddenly serious. "Hey! I think I *did* forget my toothbrush!"

Old Tom shook his head. "Toby," he said, "do you have a spare so we don't have to wait for Bad Breath Red Jon?"

"Bad Breath Red Jon," Jonathan shouted, doubling over in laughter. "I love it! But what I love even better is getting Old Tom! I was only kidding! I brought it with me!"

"Your toothbrush?"

"No! My teddy bear! Ha!"

Tom shook his head again and smiled, but he was clearly not amused by goofy Jon. "Anybody else?" Old Tom said. "Everybody got everything?"

"I don't need much." Big Dan showed those huge teeth that always looked whiter than anyone else's against his dark face. "Couple pairs of jeans and a bunch of shirts. What else is there?"

"We takin' the week off from detective work?" Little Joel asked. "Or do you have some big case for us?"

"Well," I said, "I wouldn't call it a big case, but I thought we might check out the Butchbaker place."

Joel, Dan, and Jon flinched, and even Old Tom shot me a double take.

"Not me!" Joel said. "I'll be at your house, watchin' TV!"

"You know my mom's not going to let us watch much TV," I said.

"Are you sure you want to mess with old Witch Butch-baker?" Tom asked.

"Careful," I said. "My parents don't let us call her that. Anyway, all I want to do is somehow get a good look at her. I've never really seen her face, and she's supposed to be as ugly as dirt."

"I'm not goin' anywhere near that place!" Big Dan said. "Gives me the creeps even riding by there on my bike!"

"Yeah," I said, "but the house is set way back from the street for some reason. Aren't you curious about that?"

"Who cares?" Joel said. "I vote we leave the whole thing alone."

"Me too," Red Jon said, suddenly serious. "Let's just have fun this week."

"Maybe we'll vote on it later, huh, Toby?" Tom said.

"I guess," I muttered, certain they would all chicken out. I really wanted to know about the Butchbaker place and the ugly old woman who lived there. Everybody had an idea about who she was and what she was up to, but nobody I knew really knew the truth. All I'd ever heard were rumors and scary stories.

Mrs. Butchbaker's huge old house, at the other end of the block from ours, did sit way back. The front yard seemed twice as deep as any of the others, and the house itself was the biggest on the street. I couldn't imagine why one person needed all that space.

I once mentioned that with its spires and towers it looked just like a haunted house. Of course my parents insisted there was no such thing as a haunted house.

"That looks as if it was a beautiful mansion in its day," my mother added. "It's a Victorian like ours, only bigger and older. If anything, it has more character."

Mom was always looking on the bright side of things. But then she had never been shooed away from the Butchbaker property by that old witch—I mean woman. I had, and even though Mrs. Butchbaker had never shown her face, I got the message loud and clear.

She didn't want noise. She didn't want kids. She didn't want nosy people coming around. She would tolerate you riding by, sometimes even on the sidewalk in front of her house, but stop for a second or even glance at the place, and she would wave you off. She might even raise her rake or hoe or broom, and some people said she had actually charged them, threatening to kill them.

During the first week we lived on that street, Kate and I had gone exploring, just riding around the block, looking to see if there were any other kids anywhere. Kate's sandal fell off as she was riding past the Butchbaker place, so she skidded to a stop.

The woman was working in a garden at the side of the house, and she stopped to look warily at Kate, who didn't see her at first. Just to be silly, I raced past Kate and bent over, snagging her sandal with my finger.

"Toby!" she shouted. "Bring me that! Right now!"

We had been used to living in the country and yelling all the time, not worrying about anyone's hearing us.

I rode back with the sandal, and from the garden we heard a loud *"Shhh!"*

We both jumped.

The woman turned away from us as soon as we looked at her and went back to her work.

Kate giggled, keeping an eye on the stooped old woman's back. She looked at the name on the mailbox. "That must be Mrs. Butchbaker!" she whispered. "There's a name for you!"

"Sounds German," I said.

"Sounds ugly," Kate said.

"Get off my property!" the old woman screeched, without turning to face us. "Now!"

I wanted to say that we weren't on her property, that sidewalks were city property. But neither Kate nor I wanted to find out how serious the old woman was. Maybe she just didn't want to be bothered.

The longer we lived on that street, the more stories we heard. First, we heard the woman had always lived there alone and had been there longer than anyone else in the neighborhood. Then we heard that she had been married once but had murdered her husband and buried him in the garden.

Eventually the story grew to where she had had a big family and killed them all. Some said she had eaten them. We know most of that had to be baloney, but the more we heard the scarier she became.

When I asked kids at school if they had heard of a Butchbaker woman on our street, they told me *everybody* knew about the witch.

"The witch?" I said.

"Of course! Everybody knows she's a witch!"

And then more stories erupted. Now she was a person who killed animals and ate them, then stuffed their carcasses and hung them on her wall.

"Even the police won't go near her," someone said. "Even though they know she's committed all kinds of murders and other crimes."

Well, after a while I began to realize that it couldn't all be true. And with my dad being a deputy sheriff, I knew the police stuff wasn't true. If the cops believed the old woman had committed a crime, they'd arrest her; it was as simple as that.

"I'll look her up in our records, if you're that curious," Dad told me. "All I can tell you is how long she's lived there and all that. I can't tell you any deep dark secrets if they're not part of the public record."

And so he did. "Nothing much in our files," he told me at dinner one night. "She's lived in that house more than fifty years—since her family moved here from Europe. She was one of several daughters of the Haase family, and there was one son. Apparently she's the only one who's still alive."

"Did she ever marry?" I asked.

"I'll bet you can guess," Dad said, "since her name is no longer Haase. She has an interesting first name—Hannelore."

My mother said, "That has to be German. Hannelore Butchbaker. Hmm."

"So," Kate had said, "is she a witch or not? Or is she just a murderer?"

Mom and Dad laughed but then made Kate promise she would never say such a thing outside the house.

"Neither," Dad told her. "There's nothing in the police record about any crimes ever having been committed by anyone in that house. There are lots of reports of complaints over the years, though."

"Complaints about what?"

"Prowlers, disturbances of the peace, that kind of thing. The complaints always came from someone in the house and were directed at neighbors or vandals. I guess in years past there were all kinds of incidents there. It was the favorite sport of high school kids years ago to try to scare the people in that house. They would egg the place or soap the windows, ring the doorbell and run away—that kind of stuff."

"Anything recently?" I asked.

"I wouldn't know," Dad said. "Our records stop about twenty years ago when the house became part of the city and we lost jurisdiction. But up to then, anytime high schoolers wanted to pull a prank, the Butchbaker house was the target."

"I wonder why," I said.

Dad shrugged. "Sometimes people just get it in their heads that one place is better than another to have fun with. Maybe the Butchbakers gave them what they wanted. Maybe they screamed and threatened and called the sheriff every time, making it risky to do anything to them or to their house. That just made it all the more fun."

My mother dabbed thoughtfully at her chin with her napkin and pushed her chair back a few inches, staring at my dad. "Why, Phil," she said, "you didn't really need to check all the records to know that, did you?"

"What do you mean?"

"*You* ran giggling from that property a few times yourself as a teenager, didn't you?"

"Me?"

"Yes, you! And wasn't there a Pamela Butchbaker who went to high school with us?"

"There might have been, but I don't—"

"You don't what? You felt sorry for her because no one talked to her."

"No one could understand her, Lynn," Dad said. "She had that thick accent."

"That was no reason to shun her like we did."

"We were high school kids, hon," Dad said. "We didn't know any better."

"Well, I did," Mom said. "And I felt guilty about that for a long time. Whatever became of Pamela Butchbaker?"

"I have no idea."

"Here we've been living down the block from her mother all this time and didn't even know it. I think I might just call on her."

The First Foray

My mother visited the Butchbaker home that summer. She did it the old-fashioned way. She baked a pie, covered it with a towel, and carried it down there, unannounced.

I asked her as she was leaving, "Shouldn't you call first?"

"She has to be home," Mom said. "I've never seen her anywhere but there. She has her groceries delivered."

"I know," I said. "I've seen Steve Sakay deliver them. He just leaves them near the front door. Wonder how she pays for them."

"They probably just bill her."

I followed Mom that day. I was curious. I wanted to see how Mrs. Butchbaker would react to a stranger. I stayed out of sight and leaned my bike against a tree across the street from Mrs. Butchbaker's house. I wanted to tell Mom I could see something she couldn't see, but I didn't want her to know I was snooping. I didn't think I was really doing anything wrong because I was also close enough to help if the old witch tried to boil her in a pot and eat her!

But when Mom walked up the long driveway past the deep front lawn and mounted the steps to the creaky front porch, I saw Mrs. Butchbaker hoeing in her vegetable garden. She was at the north end of her house, where my mother couldn't have seen her. The old woman didn't seem to hear her ring the bell, but I noticed her turn quickly when Mom rapped on the door. Then it appeared Mrs. Butchbaker was hurrying toward the back door.

I rode to the end of the block and came around the other way, where I could look between houses into the Butchbaker backyard. Sure enough, she had gone inside. So she must be answering the front door! I raced back around the block to where I had been.

Mom was no longer on the porch! Cool! She was in!

But she wasn't. As I watched the front door, imagining all sorts of terrible things Mrs. Butchbaker could be doing to my mother, I heard Mom calling for the old woman from the backyard. Soon Mom came around the other side of the house, looking puzzled. I had to quick straighten my bike so she wouldn't see me sticking out from either side of the tree across the street.

Mom wasn't the type to give up, and she knew as well as I did that Mrs. Butchbaker was there and that she had to have slipped in the back door. Mom kept ringing the bell and rapping on the door, then the windows. She even peered into one of them, but who knows what she saw?

Finally, when it became clear that Mrs. Butchbaker was not going to answer the door, Mom wrote a note, slipped it under the towel over the pie, and left the pie on the porch near the door.

While Mom trudged home, looking as disappointed and sad as she was irritated, I stayed put, waiting to see what, if anything, Mrs. Butchbaker would do.

I was not disappointed. I saw a curtain slightly pulled aside while she peeked out, apparently to see if Mom was finally out of sight. Then she opened the door and knelt to study the pie. She pulled away the towel, found the note, read it, smelled the pie, replaced the note and the towel, and left the pie where she found it.

I spent the rest of that week riding back and forth in front of the Butchbaker place, waiting to see if she would ever retrieve the pie. She didn't, and Mom was pretty discouraged. But on Thursday I noticed that a box of groceries from Walt's Foods was also on the porch. I hadn't seen Steve Sakay deliver it, but I stayed in the area to see how long it remained there.

Not long. Mrs. Butchbaker eventually came out and took the groceries back in, and she left the door open. What did that mean? Only that she was coming back out, and when she did, she took the pie—note, towel, and all—and moved it to the front of the porch.

I raced home to tell Mom.

"You want me to get it and bring it to you?" I asked.

"You might as well," she said with a sigh. "I at least want that good pie plate back."

I was probably bolder than I should have been, heading back down the street. But I was on a mission. That woman was cold and mean. How dare she treat my mother and her gift that way? I rode right up the driveway, across the front of the lawn, parked my bike at the bottom of the steps, and trotted up the stairs to get the pie.

Mrs. Butchbaker must have seen me coming and didn't recognize me as belonging to the pie. Just as I was reaching for it, the door flew open, and I heard a grunt and saw the flash of her broom.

"*Nein! Nein!*" she shouted.

I knew enough to know that was the German word for *no*, but I was hardly thinking about that as I tripped and staggered down the steps to my bike.

I didn't even take the time to climb aboard. I just booted up the kickstand and ran the bike down the drive and into the street. Finally I jumped on and raced away, my heart banging till I thought it would burst. Later my mother walked sadly down the street and got the now spoiled pie.

And that was the story I told the junior deputies that first night of the last week of summer before school. They were as angry as I was.

"How'd she dare do that?" Big Dan said, shaking his head. "How do you just ignore someone's kindness?"

"It was worse than that," Old Tom said. "She made it clear she didn't want it. Left it right out there at the edge of the porch so Mrs. Andrews could just come and get it."

"Unbelievable," Red Jon said. "I think we should make her pay."

We all laughed, and then we got serious. What would be the harm if we just sneaked down there and rang her doorbell? A little innocent fun! Worst of all, it was my idea.

Old Tom was silent, as he often was when we were doing something he thought was either wrong or stupid.

I didn't know whether we'd really go through with anything. But it was fun to sneak out of the house and run down the block, circling around and coming to the Butchbaker house from between the houses behind it.

What a creepy place! Every time I looked, I could make out in the darkness that Little Joel was staying pretty close to Old Tom. Neither was too excited about this adventure, but I was into it, and I assumed Red Jon and Big Dan were too. They were giggling and trying not to laugh out loud.

There was still a light on in the house, so we weren't sure it would be any fun to ring the doorbell and run. If Mrs. Butchbaker was still awake, what was the big deal? So she had to go to the door—so what?

Tom was holding back.

"What'sa matter, Old Tom?" Red Jon asked. "Don't you want to have some fun?"

"I don't know what's so fun about terrorizing an old woman," Tom said.

"Terrorizing?" Big Dan said. "If we wanted to terrorize her, we'd pretend we were prowlers—or burglars. We'd find out where her bedroom window was and scratch on it while she slept."

"We're not doing *that!*" I shouted.

"Of course not," Dan said. "I was just saying . . ."

The truth was, we knew Old Tom was right, but why did he always have to be our conscience? If we always did the right thing because it was the right thing, the way my dad always said, we'd never have any fun. "What do *you* think we should do?" I asked Tom.

"I don't know," he said. "Maybe call her a taxi or order her some pizzas. It's a fun prank. Doesn't hurt anybody."

I liked the idea, but Little Joel was thinking more clearly. "It does too hurt somebody," he said. "How about the pizza place or the cabdriver? They're going to lose money."

"You're right," Tom said. "How much money do we have? How much is it worth to us?"

We dug in our pockets and decided we had enough money to do both. It was starting to seem like a waste, though. I mean, we could eat the pizza, but by the time we paid off a cab driver, what would we have to show for it? Still, we were flushed with the excitement of it, and we decided that the cab would be the cheapest part. A cabbie would drive out from downtown, and once he found out Mrs. Butchbaker had not called him, we would give him a few bucks. It would be just like picking up a fare.

Tom's voice sounded the oldest, so he did the calling from the extension phone upstairs at our house. We had to be super quiet, coming in and going out.

Tom asked for a cab to the airport for Mrs. Butchbaker

and gave her address. "Oh, well, then," he said, "just to the store then. Yeah, the all-night grocery."

When he hung up, he was laughing. "I don't know if they bought it," he said. "They said there weren't any more planes out of Kalamazoo Municipal this time of night. I switched to the grocery store, and they said they assumed I meant the all-night grocery."

"So are they coming?"

"I don't know. I think so."

"Let's go!"

"What about the pizza?" Big Dan said.

Tom called a local pizzeria and ordered two large pies with everything. Then it was back to the bushes at the side of the Butchbaker place. We got there about five minutes before the cab pulled up.

We poked each other and giggled as the cab sat out in front of the house, waiting patiently. Little Joel scampered around front and came back to report that he thought he had seen the curtain move in the lighted upstairs bedroom.

"Mrs. Butchbaker must be wondering what in the world is goin' on!" Red Jon said.

Then we heard the cabbie tap his horn. A few minutes later he tapped it again, and then twice. Within a minute he was leaning on the horn, and lights were coming on all over the neighborhood. Finally someone opened a window and hollered, "Shut up down there!"

With that the cabbie backed up and drove into the driveway, shining his spotlight on the house number, on the front door, on each window, and finally into the lighted window upstairs. That light went off, and we guessed he assumed that meant Mrs. Butchbaker was finally ready and would be coming down. But of course she didn't.

Next we heard him come charging out of the cab, slamming the door and grumbling loudly. He stomped up the steps, marched across the porch to the door, and rang the bell.

Then twice. Then three times. Eventually he banged and banged on the door, finally hollering, "Mrs. Butchbaker, I know you're in there! Don't call a cab and then stiff me! Who's gonna pay for this?"

Tom shifted uncomfortably beside me, and I knew he couldn't take it any more. "Hey, buddy," he whispered, and the cabbie jumped. "We'll pay you for your trouble."

The cabbie moved to the side of the porch, where he saw us all huddled in the bushes across the driveway. "So this was a prank, huh?" he said. "It's going to cost you."

"That's all right," Red Jon said, giggling. "It was worth it."

"I pulled this a few times when I was a kid," the cabbie said, taking our money but surprisingly not much of it. "I don't think I ever owned up to it and paid, though."

"We probably shouldn't have either," Big Dan said, smiling.

"This is a first for me," the cabbie said, "but I appreciate it. I've been stiffed and pranked a lot of times, and it's hard enough to make a living at this as it is."

He wasn't gone three minutes when the pizza delivery car slid up the driveway and a husky, blonde girl of about twenty hopped out, carrying the insulated container with two large pizzas in it.

She was all business, slamming the car door and bounding up the steps. She rang the bell and stood there rocking on the balls of her feet, whistling. She looked at her watch, rang the bell a few more times, knocked, and called out, "Pizza! Mrs. Butchbaker! Pizza!"

We couldn't keep from laughing. We laughed so hard we scared the pizza girl.

"We'll take those off your hands," Red Jon finally blurted.

"You'll have to fight me for 'em," she said, straightening to her full height and looking as if she could take on all of us at once.

"No," I said. "We'll buy them. We ordered them. It was just a joke to have you bring them here."

"So Mrs. Butchbaker didn't order these."

"Right."

"That's a relief. I couldn't imagine what an old widow woman would do with two larges in the first place!"

We were afraid the smell of the pizzas would wake my parents, so we ate them in my backyard and sneaked into the kitchen for Cokes. We got talking and laughing too loud, and pretty soon my mother called out from the master bedroom, "You guys get upstairs to bed right now!"

"Yes, ma'am!" I said, and we all charged into the house and up the stairs, laughing.

We didn't get much satisfaction paying back Mrs. Butchbaker for thumbing her nose at Mom's gift and gesture of kindness. And, unfortunately, the mystery of the old witch remained.

The Investigation Begins

The next day it was time to get down to business. We borrowed my dad's camera with the telephoto lens, and the guys went off to try to get pictures of the face we had never really seen. I assigned myself the task of talking with Steve Sakay.

Steve's parents owned Walt's Foods, and he'd been a stock and bag boy and had been delivering groceries there for years. I knew him because his mother had been my teacher in third grade, and he used to help her on field trips. We were friends.

"I'm curious about Mrs. Butchbaker," I told him as he was bagging groceries.

"So am I," he said. "She tips me every time, and I get a Christmas card with a little cash in it each year, but I've never seen her. Her order is left in an envelope on the porch, and Dad bills her by mail. She always pays immediately."

"All these years and you've never seen her?"

"A couple of times by accident. She might not realize I'm

there and open the door to get her mail or something. I try to greet her, but she always just turns and goes back in."

"Is she as ugly as people say?"

"She's pretty ugly."

"Mean?"

"Not to me. Of course, I get the message loud and clear that she doesn't want to see me or greet me or have me see her or greet her in any way. Once I was driving by, and she was raking leaves out on the parkway. I honked and waved, and I know she saw me, but she didn't even pretend to notice."

"What do you make of it, Steve?"

"I don't know. I've heard all the stories. Killed her whole family, buried 'em in there or ate 'em, or something."

"Pretty wild."

"Yeah. I don't believe any of that. Something's going on, though. Why would a woman be such a recluse?"

"What's a recluse?"

"A hermit. Keeps to herself so much."

I shrugged. That's what I was trying to find out. "Thanks, anyway, Steve."

"Hey," he said as I was leaving. "Have you thought of old Mrs. Lawrence?"

"What about her?"

"She couldn't be too much younger than Mrs. Butchbaker. I'll bet she remembers when they were both younger. She might even remember what it was like at the Butchbaker place when the Lawrences moved in."

"Maybe," I said.

By the time I got back to my block, I couldn't find the guys anywhere. I rode downtown and found them hanging around the one-hour photo processing store.

"We got some great stuff," Old Tom said. "I didn't know how much fun that camera could be."

I was surprised he wasn't already feeling guilty about

shooting pictures from a hiding place. "What'd you get?"

"She was out in the yard again," Red Jon said. "Feeding the birds or something, which is kind of strange because she's always shooing away cats and dogs. Tom was just firing away and giving us a peek now and then through that long lens. She sure is ugly."

"She can't help that," Tom said. "None of us are real prizes either."

"I am!" Little Joel blurted. "At least my mom thinks so!"

The pictures didn't turn out as great as Tom and the others thought they would. He had forgotten to turn on the automatic focus for some of them, and he didn't know how to focus the camera manually. Still, these were the clearest looks we had ever had at the homely face of the old woman. Her face was pasty white with a pointy chin and sharp cheekbones. She had dark, bushy eyebrows and white hair sticking out of her hooded sweatshirt. Her mouth seemed frozen in a scowl. There really was a witchlike quality to her look.

"These just make me more curious," I said.

"Me too," Old Tom said. "What would make a person so miserable looking?"

I told them that Steve Sakay suggested I talk to Mrs. Lawrence.

"The woman who lives near you who remembers the mobsters that used to live in your house?"

"She's the one."

"You're the only one who knows her," Tom said. "You're elected again."

I didn't mind. I always liked talking with Mrs. Lawrence. I knew that she napped in the early afternoon, so I waited until just before dinner when the guys got tired of spying on the Butchbaker place. They were all at my house, just hanging out and meeting in the old coal bin when I rang Mrs. Lawrence's doorbell.

I didn't want her to have to work her way out of her chair

before the TV and hobble to the door, so as soon as I heard her mute the TV, I called out to tell her who I was.

"Oh, come right in, Tobin!" she said.

I hated when she called me by my full name, but she insisted on doing that to everyone—even my parents, whom she called Philip and Lynette.

"Can I get you anything? A soda? Some fruit?"

I declined everything, though it sounded good. I knew she didn't really want to get up and get it, and I wasn't supposed to spoil my appetite before dinner anyway.

"What's on your mind?" she said at last. "And can it wait until my program is over?"

"It'll wait," I said, and she immediately turned the sound back on to finish watching one of her favorite game shows.

I had done enough odd jobs for her to know that she loved her TV. Beside napping, it was pretty much all she did all day—watch a bunch of favorites on lots of different channels. Her grown son, who lived a few blocks away, visited her just after dinner each night to make sure she was all right and had everything she needed. That seemed to be what she scheduled her day around.

I shoveled her driveway and her walk and cut her grass, and she always gave me one dollar and said every time, "Keep the change, and don't spend it all in one place."

Her son explained that she was way behind the times moneywise, and he paid me what the jobs were worth and said her dollar was really just the tip.

"Still got all those dollars?" she would ask me now and then.

"Yes, ma'am," I'd say.

And she'd say, "Good! Put yourself through college someday!"

When her show was finally over, she announced, "I've got half an hour just for you. Lucky for you, there's nothing on but trash until five, so what do you want?"

"I want to talk about the Butchbakers," I said.

She fixed a dark gaze on me. "And why would you want to do that?"

"I've heard all the stories. I just want the truth."

"And what makes you think the stories aren't true?"

"Have you heard the same stories I have?" I asked.

"You mean about all the witchcraft and the murders and the cannibalism?"

I nodded.

"Course I have. Who hasn't? Those make for good bedtime stories if you want to be scared out of your wits, but only a fool believes them. You don't, do you?"

I thought I had just implied that, but I shook my head anyway. Anything to keep her talking. "How well do you remember the Butchbakers? They were here when you moved in, weren't they?"

"Child, they were the Haases then, and they were here when everybody moved in. And as for my memory, it's good and bad. I can't remember what happened yesterday, but I can remember ten, twenty, fifty years ago like it was this morning. Imagine that. Half the time I can watch a rerun of one of my shows and not realize it's a rerun until halfway through. Makes me feel like a crazy old fool."

"You're certainly not that!" I said.

"Bless you," she said. "Now what were we talking about?"

I started to tell her, but she laughed really loud and said, "C'mon, Tobin! Can't you take a joke? My memory's not so bad I can't remember from one minute to the next!"

I smiled as if I thought she had been real funny.

"Now, the Butchbakers," she said. "The woman wasn't a Butchbaker until she married John Butchbaker comin' on to fifty years ago now. I was in that wedding."

"You were a friend of hers?"

"Sort of. We went to the same school."

"Are you still her friend?"

"Nobody's still her friend, Tobin. Don't you know that?"

"I guess I do, but why?"

"I'll get to that," she said, "but don't you want me to start from the beginning?"

"Sure," I said. Did I ever! But I didn't want to be there all day either. I tried to sneak a peek at my watch, but she noticed.

"Don't worry, son," she said. "You're out of here when my next show comes on anyway!"

I laughed, and she began.

"The way I understand it," she said, "the Haase family moved here from Germany in the middle nineteen forties. They were all crammed into a little apartment building over their five-and-dime on Burdick Street downtown. You know what a five-and-dime is?"

"Not really."

"Why do you kids say that all the time? Either you do or you don't. You know what a five-and-dime store is or not?"

"I've heard my mom talk about dime stores," I said, "but I can't imagine buying anything for a dime."

"Well, back then you could buy some things for a penny or two, and a five-and-dime was a store where you bought little notions." And rather than ask me if I knew what a notion was, she just told me. "Notions are things you buy on impulse. You don't know you need it or want it until you see it. Little stuff. Toys and necessities."

I nodded, just to keep her moving on the story. I didn't much care what the Haases sold in their five-and-dime fifty years before. I was more interested in how they wound up on our street and why one of the daughters became an ugly, ornery old witch.

"I guess things were pretty hard for them at first," Mrs. Lawrence said. "It seems Mr. Haase had been big in the lumber business in Germany before the war, so this was quite a comedown for them. They had to live in a tiny place and take over the small store business. The whole family worked there, but Mr. Haase was busy making some deals. Whether he had smuggled some money out of Germany before they got here or made a killing on the stock market, I don't know. All I know is, one day they bought a big piece of land here—where that house is now—and started building that huge Victorian. You know what a Victorian is, of course. You live in one."

"Yes, ma'am."

Now it was Mrs. Lawrence's turn to look at the clock. "We may have to finish this another time," she said, "but let me keep going. You should see the inside of that house."

"I'd love to."

"You probably never will, long as she's alive. I don't think there's been another living soul in there for more than twenty years, but I'm gettin' ahead of myself. The lumber for that place was delivered by one of the local lumber companies, but it wasn't their lumber. It was imported."

"Why would anybody need to import lumber into Michigan?" I asked, knowing that we were a big lumber state and one of the furniture-making capitals of the world.

"That's just it," Mrs. Lawrence said, grabbing the cane that had been leaning against her chair and giving it a rap on the floor for emphasis. "It was only the best for Friedrich Haase. Some of that wood was rumored to have been shipped in from the Black Forest."

"All the way from Germany?"

"All the way. And some of the marble tile was imported from Italy."

"Marble tile in a house in this neighborhood?" I said. Ceramic, rubber, linoleum maybe—but marble?

"That's what I'm tellin' you, Tobin. That house was a mansion the day it was built, and it's still probably the most valuable property in this part of town. My family and I lived way west of Woods Street back then, and we would walk over here just to see the thing going up."

"That must have been cool."

"No," she said flatly, "it was in the late spring and summer, so it mostly wasn't cool at all."

"No, I mean it must have been pretty neat."

"Well, it *was* neat when it was finished, but during the building of it, even with Friedrich Haase there supervising, it wasn't neat at all. It was a big mess, like most building projects are."

More Revelations

I sat there trying to hide my smile, but Mrs. Lawrence had been teasing me again.

"You really think I don't know what 'cool' and 'neat' mean, Tobin?"

"I figured you did," I said, laughing.

"You did not! I got you good!"

"Yes, ma'am," I said, smiling. "You did."

She really enjoyed that and muttered to herself, "Young people think they've got a corner on brains. Anyway, Tobin, like I say, Star Haase and I went to school together."

"That old woman's name is Star?"

"I don't know what her name was in German, but that's the name she went by when we were in school."

"Grade school?"

Mrs. Lawrence threw her head back and laughed loud. "Thank you, child!" she said. "How young do you think I am?"

"I don't know," I said. "Fifty years ago you weren't still in grade school?"

"Heavens, no! I was in my late twenties fifty years ago, going to secretarial school."

"That's where you met Mrs. Butchbaker?"

"Star Haase, yes. And quiet? My, she was quiet."

"But you were friends?"

"As much as anyone can be a friend of a Haase. They kept to themselves and didn't talk much."

"Any idea why?"

"Something must have happened to them in Germany—that's all I can imagine."

I was disappointed that Mrs. Lawrence seemed to be only guessing. "But you don't know for sure?"

"I know," she said, seeming to study the quiet television where some silly show was on.

"And you're not going to tell me?"

"I'm thinking about it, Tobin. She was such a sad, sad girl."

I wanted to ask why, but apparently she was going to tell me in her own time.

"It's almost time for my show," she said softly.

"Would you mind if I came back tomorrow?"

"On one condition. You look up the history of Germany in the nineteen forties, and you tell me what might have happened to the Haases."

"Where will I find that?"

"That's your problem, isn't it, Tobin?"

The guys weren't too happy about how little I found out from Mrs. Lawrence.

"She had a different name before she was married, and her dad built the first house in the neighborhood. Big deal," Big Dan said. "We could assume the first and guess the second because of the size of the house and where it lies on the lot."

"I'm losing interest in this Butchbaker woman," Red Jon said.

"Me too," Old Tom said.

"I haven't lost interest," Dan said, his dark eyes flashing. "But I don't care that much about her history."

I couldn't believe it. I was hooked and wanted to learn all I could about the woman. I wanted to see her up close, and in a way I hoped there were bodies buried in that house. But I didn't want to force the guys to investigate something they didn't care about.

"I'd rather just play more practical jokes on her," Little Joel said. Little Joel, of all people!

We all turned and stared at him.

"I thought you were scared to death of her and that house," Old Tom said.

"I am!" Joel said. "That's what's fun about it. I wouldn't even mind bein' used as bait!"

"Bait?" Red Jon said. "Like makin' her chase you past us so we can get a look at her?"

"Yeah!"

"No way!" Tom said. "Somewhere we have to draw the line. I mean, what's the point of all this? It's too easy, scaring an old, defenseless woman. She can't catch us, can't hurt us, probably can't even get us into trouble. Is this what we're all about?"

It wasn't, of course, but it sure sounded like fun.

I didn't want to be a killjoy, so I waited until everybody else was in bed and had stopped whispering before I got to my computer and called up the encyclopedia on the Internet. I didn't want to waste a lot of time and money staying on-line, so I just clicked off all the entries on Germany from the 1930s and 1940s, downloaded them into a file, and got off the Internet. Then I printed them out and took them back to bed with a flashlight.

By the time I got in there, Big Dan, Red Jon, and Little Joel were sound asleep, breathing deeply.

Tom was on his back in a sleeping bag, his hands behind

his head, eyes open. He had told me once that he always tried to stay awake when he was at my place, because he enjoyed the freedom so much. "When I'm asleep, I might as well be back at Lake Farm in a big dorm full of bunk beds," he said. "So when I'm here I like to look around and realize I'm safe and free."

I nodded to him as I tiptoed in.

"Whad'ya find?" he asked.

"I'm not sure yet," I whispered. "There was lots of stuff."

"Let's see," he said, rolling out of his bag. "Do you mind?"

"Nope." In fact, I was glad someone else would be reading the stuff with me.

We sat at my desk and tried to read in the narrow, dim beam of the flashlight. I had heard of Adolf Hitler, of course, but I had never read anything like what I was seeing that night.

We'd learned in school that Adolf Hitler was a dictator. He was the leader of Germany and head of the Nazi political party, which believed that Jews and gypsies were inferior and that only the white race was worthy of power and privilege. But what I read in the electronic encyclopedia taught me so much more that I realized I would never be the same.

Old Tom and I said nothing to each other as we read, but I think we both knew we were learning something that most people didn't learn until they were older.

The encyclopedia told a frightening story. It said that Hitler and his Nazis went so far as to arrest and put in prison and kill Jews and other minorities. He believed they did not have the right to live.

I wondered how that could have been possible. The encyclopedia told of Jews who tried to hide from the Nazis. Other Germans helped them and got arrested themselves. Was this what Mrs. Lawrence wanted me to read about the Haases?

I knew Mrs. Lawrence was a little younger than Mrs. Butchbaker. So when Mrs. Butchbaker was Star Haase—still living in Germany—she would have been in her twenties during the rise of Adolf Hitler. Could Mrs. Butchbaker have been a Jew when she was a Haase? Could her family have been imprisoned? Or were she and her family Nazis? Or Germans who protected Jews from the Nazis? I had to know.

In the morning, Big Dan said he had been doing some calculations. He said that if we wanted to be able to see inside Mrs. Butchbaker's house without being seen by her or anyone else, we would have to do it late in the afternoon.

"The sun dips under the awning on her side window," he said, "but there's still a shadow outside. If we stand in the shadow, we can see inside without her seeing us, unless she's in that room or outside. And no one from the street should be able to see us at that time of day if we wait in the bushes on the other side of her driveway and move to the window when no one's driving or walking by."

The rest of the guys liked that plan, because it meant they didn't have to worry about Mrs. Butchbaker until late that afternoon. In their minds there was nothing to do until then except play and have fun. I should have been a better host and found things for them to do, but both Old Tom and I had the same idea. We were going to the library.

I told the guys to stay out of my mom's hair, ride their bikes to the school, play ball, play in the old coal bin, whatever. "Tom and I will be at the library. We're onto something."

"The *library!*" Big Dan said. "That sounds too much like school! Have fun!"

Actually Tom and I did have fun. I found a bunch of books about the Nazis and the Luftwaffe (the German air force). I got so interested in their weapons and tactics that I almost forgot what I was looking for.

Occasionally I stopped to think how strange it was that I

should so enjoy being in a library. My parents and my teachers had been trying to convince me for years that there was a gold mine of fascinating information here. But I had been too busy having fun and believing the myths about libraries. I thought it was all old boring stuff.

Well, what I was reading now was old all right, but it sure wasn't boring. I had never known or cared much about Germany, but when I realized I was reading about a place and a period my neighbor had lived in and through, I couldn't get enough of it.

Hitler had tried to rise to power long before he succeeded. He was in prison for a while and wrote a book called *Mein Kampf,* which means *My Plan.* Even the people of Germany at first thought his ideas were bigoted and hateful and crazy. But when the time was right, when they were ready for something and someone new, someone who would bring back the pride of the fatherland, he surged to power. He was a great speaker who could whip crowds into a frenzy of excitement and loyalty, and soon the Nazi party was in complete control of Germany.

Hitler used his storm troopers to enforce his ideas. You were either loyal to him, or you were imprisoned and possibly put to death. Jews were rounded up and shipped to labor and death camps. The answer to the problem of the Jews, he said, was to rid Germany of their evil influence. He believed they were inferior and that they would weaken the race.

Millions of Jews were sent to these camps in crowded boxcars. Then they were forced to work in horrible conditions and were given barely enough food to keep them alive, their bodies beginning to look like living skeletons with just skin stretched across the bones. The pictures of men, women, and even children wasting away, their dark, sad, defeated eyes peering at the camera, made me want to cry.

The Nazis were so convinced of the worthlessness of their

Jewish prisoners that they even used them for medical experiments. Before some prisoners were killed, they were heated, frozen, operated on, had body parts cut off, and whatever else the Nazis wanted to do to them. The Nazis believed that the best service the Jews could provide the rest of Germany was to serve as experiments.

Worst of all, when the imprisoned Jews were finally useless to the Nazis, when they were too weak and sick to work, they were herded into showers that weren't really showers at all. They were gas chambers where the Jews were poisoned to death. Then they were carried to the crematorium, where their bodies were burned to ashes.

I sat there shaking my head, reading all this stuff. I had heard about six million Jews being put to death by Hitler in World War Two, but it had never made an impression on me. All that had seemed so long ago and so far away. But now, knowing that someone I had seen with my own eyes had to have been there when it happened and somehow lived through it, well, that made it come to life for me.

I couldn't wait to ask Mrs. Lawrence what else she knew about Star Haase Butchbaker. Had she been a follower of Hitler? An enemy? A protector of Jews? And what about her father?

Meanwhile, Old Tom had found microfilm and microfiche of the *Kalamazoo Gazette* and the *Detroit Free Press* from the 1930s and 1940s, and what he found started to get us closer to the truth about the Haases and the Butchbakers.

He called me over, and I stood behind him as he rolled the microfilm into the viewer and we saw page after page of news flash by. It took most of the day to look through all the news pages and find mentions of the Haase family, which had moved into Kalamazoo from Germany and finally from downtown to our own community.

Tom found the first mention of the move. In an index, he looked up the name "Haase, Friedrich," and it pointed him to a page of the *Gazette* in the mid-1940s, when the family first arrived in Michigan. I read it carefully to see why they would have come here in the first place.

The First Peek at Truth

The first article Old Tom and I found was a simple story of a German lumberyard owner who had emigrated to South America, then moved to the United States—specifically to Kalamazoo—to try to build a lumber business here.

Why he started with a five-and-dime store, I didn't know. How he made enough money at that to start his lumber business and build a big house in the middle of nowhere (which was now my neighborhood) I couldn't figure either.

At the time of the first article, Mr. Haase had just moved his family into a cramped apartment downtown and had bought the five-and-dime. But he was quoted as saying that he had been a lumberman in Germany and wanted to do the same here. It must have seemed to readers of the *Gazette* that this was just a dream. But a feature story less than a year later told of his selling the five-and-dime and buying a lumberyard.

The story also showed the foundation going up on his huge new home. And that was where the mystery really began. The reporter had discovered that the Haases had not really come directly from Germany but had spent a few years in South America. When asked about that, Friedrich Haase said they had been merely visiting relatives, but records showed that the visit had lasted several years.

All during the time the house was being built, controversy raged in the daily newspaper about who Friedrich Haase really was. Many friends and acquaintances and business associates supported him, telling how nice a guy and what an honest businessman he was. Others questioned how he could have made so much money so fast.

The real problems came when some suggested that because he and his family were from Germany, and Germany was terrorizing all of Europe under Hitler's command, Friedrich Haase should be looked upon with suspicion.

The newspaper showed pictures of swastikas, the German symbol for Nazism, painted on the house builder's sign and on the plywood frame as the building was begun. The original builder eventually backed away from the project as more people began suspecting that Haase had been a Nazi.

As Old Tom and I studied the newspaper articles, though, we couldn't make the dates work. Even if Friedrich Haase had been in the military, he seemed to have left Germany long before the worst of Hitler's acts.

We left the library silently, only later talking about all that we had read. It seemed to me I had learned more history, just trying to figure out a strange woman, than I had in all my years of school. I loved looking up that stuff and finding clues! I never dreamed that I would enjoy something that seemed so much like schoolwork. But when there was a present-day connection, like the puzzling Mrs. Butchbaker, it was all that much more interesting.

Tom and the others ventured out that afternoon to see what they could see at the Butchbaker place. Knowing that the house had been vandalized more than fifty years before by people painting swastikas on the property, we warned Jon and Big Dan and Joel not to do anything to scare the old woman. She would have been in her twenties when that stuff happened, and there was no sense in bringing back bad memories.

Meanwhile, I had an appointment with Mrs. Lawrence, which she somehow remembered and even seemed to be looking forward to.

"Splendid, Tobin!" she kept repeating. "Splendid! You did your job! You studied, and you learned. Doesn't that make more sense than just wondering whether someone is a witch?"

"I guess."

"You guess? Come now, son. You're brighter than that. You know knowledge is the key to understanding. It's only those things we don't understand that we fear. So you discovered what? That Mrs. Butchbaker—when she was Star Haase—lived in Germany in the nineteen thirties. What did that tell you?"

"That she was there during the rise of Hitler and Nazism."

"There, see? How much did you know about Hitler or Nazism before this morning?"

"Not much."

"There you go. What must it have been like for a young girl to grow up there and then?"

"That depends," I said.

"It sure does!" Mrs. Lawrence exulted, as if she knew where I was going with that logic. "And what does it depend upon?"

"On whether her family was with Hitler or against him."

"Right! And who was for him?"

"Almost everybody at first."

"Exactly. And who was against him?"

"Jews and friends of Jews."

Mrs. Lawrence sat there beaming as if I were her prize

pupil. "And what did the people of Kalamazoo think of the Haases when they first moved in?"

"Nobody knew much about them when they were running the five-and-dime. But as soon as they started to build a big house, people got suspicious."

"Why?"

"I don't know. I guess because no one knew how they could afford it."

"So what happened?"

"People painted swastikas on their house."

Mrs. Lawrence shifted in her chair and leaned forward. "What do you make of that? What were they saying about the Haases?"

"I have no idea."

"Then you must study some more."

"I'm just saying I don't know if they thought the Haases were Nazis or Jews."

"Ah, very good. If they were Nazis, decent people might want to punish them for what they did to innocent people throughout Europe. Maybe the vandals thought they were exposing the Haases as Nazis by painting swastikas on their house. But if the Haases were Jews, then people who were anti-Semitic might—you know what that means?"

"No."

"Prejudiced against Jews. People who hated Jews might have painted the swastikas as threats, trying to scare them away."

"Well," I said, "were the Haases Jews or Nazis?"

"They didn't have to be either, did they? They could have simply been German citizens who fled the danger. But the fact that they came here not directly from Germany but through South America is another clue."

"A clue to what?"

Mrs. Lawrence seemed to be trying to keep from grinning broadly. "A clue to their identity," she said. "You have more

44

homework to do. Who are these people? Why did they come here? Who were they? Why were they in South America first? If Mr. Haase was only a lumberman, why did he flee Germany? Or *was* he fleeing? Maybe he simply moved for better business opportunities. But to South America? And then here? Questions. Many questions."

"And you're going to tell me nothing?" I said.

"Of course not! This is too much fun! You are becoming a student of history, and your knowledge will free your mind. You know the Bible says that you shall know the truth and the truth shall set you free. That's talking about the truth about Christ, but all truth is God's truth, isn't it?"

I nodded. This old woman still remembered her Bible, even though she hadn't been able to get out to church for years.

She continued. "Any truth will change you. The more you know, the more you understand. What do you know about Mrs. Butchbaker that you didn't know last week?"

I shook my head. I knew more than I ever dreamed. "I didn't know you two had been friends, for one thing."

"'Friends' is overstating it a little."

"But you were in her wedding."

"They needed a witness. She knew me. That was it. I never liked John Butchbaker, and if I had known Star better I would have warned her not to marry him. But I was young, and times were different. We didn't tell each other how to live and what to do back then. I was an acquaintance, a school-mate in business college."

"You didn't run together?"

"Run? Nobody ran back then."

"I mean hang around together."

"Oh, no, not much. Just back and forth from the neighborhood to school."

"By bus?"

"Yes. That's how we met. I kept seeing her at the bus

stop, and then one day I realized we were both getting off at the same stop and getting back on the bus at the same time. I finally asked her, 'Are you going to secretarial school too?' She nodded and smiled shyly. I said, 'Cat got your tongue?' That was what we used to say to people who didn't talk. 'No,' she said softly in that thick, thick accent of hers. 'I sit behind you in typing class.'

"Well, I was so embarrassed I just laughed out loud and apologized for not having noticed. She told me she didn't notice too many people either. We started sitting together on the bus and talking a little more every day. I remember the day she met John Butchbaker. It seemed to me the only thing they had in common was that they were both German."

I didn't want to hear about John Butchbaker just yet. "Was she ugly even back then?"

"You find her ugly now?"

"I've never really seen her close up myself," I said. "But I've seen pictures, and yeah, she's pretty ugly."

"Is age ugly to you, Tobin? Am I ugly to you?"

I didn't know what to say. If Mrs. Lawrence had asked me if I thought she was pretty, I wasn't going to lie. But I could say honestly that I didn't find Mrs. Lawrence ugly. Her face was full and round, and her eyes looked tired and puffy. She was pale, except for one large, light brown mole. Her hair was white and thin and wispy, and she wore a robe all day every day.

"Well, Tobin? Are all old people ugly to you?"

"You're not ugly, ma'am. I sure wouldn't say that. No."

"Well, that's mighty generous of you."

I could tell I had offended her by calling her old friend ugly. "I guess I shouldn't have said she's exactly ugly," I said, "but I've heard the rumors about her being a witch for so long that I guess I think she looks a little like one."

"The woman is in her late seventies!" Mrs. Lawrence said. "You can't expect her to look like a movie star."

"I know."

"The more you get to know about her, the more you'll know that the years have not been kind to her. She had wonderful, soft features when she was a younger woman. I always thought she was a head-turning beauty. There was a softness about her, a shyness that was appealing. A nice shy smile. She was wonderfully trim and attractive that way."

"I'm sorry I said she was ugly."

"Well," Mrs. Lawrence said, looking out the window suddenly and talking as if I weren't there. "I suppose hard lines *have* come to her face. As the skin becomes less elastic and the elements attack the body, she's become stooped. The lines in her face have become harsher. Her eyes are colder, her cheeks sunken, her chin more pronounced. But how sad to be called a witch because of the look of one's face! Shouldn't she be judged by her character rather than by what the ravages of time have done to her appearance?"

"Of course," I said, feeling stupid and childish.

"She may not let you get to know her," Mrs. Lawrence said, "but anything more you can learn *about* her will set your mind free. You may not like her. You may not admire her. You may not want to become her friend. But if you can understand her a little more, you might be less inclined to fear her or think her a witch, don't you think?"

I nodded, knowing that my friends were sneaking around Mrs. Butchbaker's house right then, trying to get a look at her through the window from where she couldn't see them. She deserved her privacy. I didn't know yet whether she had been a victim or a villain in Germany before her family fled to South America and then to Kalamazoo. But no matter what, she didn't deserve to be treated with suspicion and contempt by a bunch of kids.

Fun as it was to pretend we were investigating a wicked witch, we were probably just hassling a lonely old woman.

Mrs. Lawrence's cane tapping on the floor brought me

back to the present. "It's time for my program," she said. "Time for you to go. Good first day of research. Same time, same place tomorrow?"

I felt guilty. I wanted to learn more, and I wanted to come back and bounce it off Mrs. Lawrence, but I also wanted to get a peek into that Butchbaker house. "Could we do it a little later?" I said.

"Sure," she said, looking at her TV listings in the paper. "At seven tomorrow night I have a half hour. That should give you lots of time to study."

The First Peek Inside

O h, man, Toby, you shoulda been there!" Red Jon said, shaking his head and grinning that pale-faced, freckled smile of his. "We got the greatest look inside that house."

I was jealous, figuring I had missed out on something. But I was still feeling guilty about our prowling around Mrs. Butchbaker's property, especially with all the new stuff I was learning about her.

"Did you see her?" I asked.

"No," Big Dan said. "But we saw plenty. And if we can somehow get her to come into that parlor at the right time of day, we can get a perfect look at her."

"What did you see?"

"All kinds of German stuff!" Little Joel said. "It was cool."

"German stuff?"

"A German flag. A map in a frame on the wall. Some steins—you know, those big mugs they drink beer out of."

"They drink everything out of them," Old Tom said.

"Whatever."

I knew Tom was sitting on the news he and I had dug out of the library. "What did *you* think?" I asked him.

"Looked like a lot of German stuff, all right," he said. "And she's a really neat housekeeper."

"Yeah!" Jon said. "For a witch! Maybe she makes her lamp shades out of human skin!"

Joel and Dan laughed, but Tom and I just looked at each other. We were losing the fun of the investigation. We had found information that sobered us. I couldn't speak for him, but I wasn't feeling right about how we were going about this.

I tried Mrs. Lawrence's argument on the rest of them. "What do you say we just look for clues about her in the old newspapers and documents at the library?"

"Nah!" they said, almost in unison. "You and Tom can do the hard stuff. We'll be the recon unit."

"You're not going to do anything stupid, are you?"

Big Dan looked offended. "Like what? Ring her doorbell and run away? That's not stupid. That's fun. Anyway, we like the idea of using Joel as bait like he suggested. We know she doesn't answer the door, but we think she peeks out from somewhere to see who it is. Tomorrow at the same time we're going to have Joel ring the doorbell and keep ringing it, and the rest of us will be at the window by the parlor. She'll have to come through there—we think—to get a look at the front door to see who's there."

I didn't know what to think. This wasn't as much fun as it had been, but I wouldn't mind getting a peek at her too. "No crazy stuff," I said. "No scaring her or anything."

"What?" Big Dan said. "Is she your new girlfriend or something?"

That made everyone howl, including Tom.

"No!" Red Jon said. "He's sweet on Mrs. Lawrence right now."

I had to smile, but I felt as if I were having to grow up too soon.

Wednesday afternoon I was hiding in the bushes across the driveway from the Butchbaker home. Old Tom was next to me, Big Dan's brown face on the other side. Red Jon crouched in front of us, and Little Joel was at the front door.

We had all agreed that he would not just run away if she answered the door. He would offer to have us do some yard work for her or something. There was no way we were going to have him just tease her or make fun of her, especially after what Tom and I had learned earlier that day.

We'd spent the morning in the library again and the afternoon in the morgue of the newspaper office. That's what they call the place where they store all their old newspapers, articles, photos, and microfilm.

Somehow Dan had determined that Mrs. Butchbaker had gone from the shed in the backyard through the back door and upstairs. We weren't sure which room upstairs was her bedroom, but we were pretty sure it was the window on the left side of the house as you faced the front. From there she would not be able to see us across the driveway or see the front door. If she was curious enough about who was there, she would have to come downstairs and go through the parlor to get to the front door or look out the parlor window onto the front porch.

"Maybe she's taking a nap," I whispered. "We should leave her be."

"Don't be a wuss," Red Jon said. "The plan's in place. Let's go through with it. You want to get a real, live, up-close look at her or not?"

I wasn't so sure.

Red Jon continued. "We're only gonna get a little glimpse at her as she walks by anyway. If she tries looking out the window where we are, she'll see us and probably turn away."

Little Joel ran to the edge of the porch, and we could hear

his clomping feet the whole way. He leaned over and stared at us. "Ready?" he whispered.

We nodded and waved that he should get back to the door and ring the bell or knock or do whatever he thought would get Mrs. Butchbaker's attention.

"Somebody should get down the driveway a little and see if her curtain moves," Dan said.

"Not you," Red Jon said. "She could see you from Mars."

"Thanks a lot," Dan said. "You're elected. Just don't let that red hair reflect from the sun and blind the old witch."

That was funny, but I winced. Already I knew a little about Mrs. Butchbaker, and that was enough to make me want to quit calling her a witch.

Red Jon slithered out of the bushes and moved toward the street, ducking back into another hedge farther down. Little Joel was ringing the doorbell. We looked at Red Jon. He was shaking his head. Nothing yet.

Finally Little Joel began knocking. Still nothing. Then he began calling out, "Mrs. Butchbaker! Mrs. Butchbaker!"

We looked at Red Jon again. He waved at us. *Success!* Something was happening upstairs. She must have pulled back the curtain to see what she could see, which was nothing—although if she had known where to look, she might have noticed Red Jon crouched in the hedge down the driveway. He was comically hugging the branches, maybe holding his breath, trying not to move an inch. We could hardly keep from giggling.

Mrs. Butchbaker must have let the curtain fall back into place, because Red Jon whispered loudly. "Now, move! Joel, keep knocking and yelling!"

Jon came up the driveway, and we crept out of the bushes, moving toward the window that looked into the parlor. Because we must have been a little earlier than the day before, the way the sunlight glared off the window we couldn't see a thing. I could, however, hear slow, labored footsteps coming down the stairs inside.

"Are you sure she has to come through here?" I whispered.

"Absolutely," Red Jon said.

I moved closer to the window and put my right hand on the pane, almost pressing my nose to the glass. The blind was down. Maybe I could see a little through a slit at the bottom. Red Jon was just off my left shoulder. Old Tom was towering over both of us from behind, and Big Dan was to Jon's left. I could hear Joel clomping down off the porch to join us.

"What's he doing?" Red Jon demanded. "He should stay there!"

When Joel got to us, Dan shushed him just as the blind shot up and Mrs. Butchbaker came into view. Because of the glare, she couldn't see us at first, and we stood there, staring into her face.

Regardless of what Mrs. Lawrence had said, this was an ugly woman. As her dark, fearful eyes adjusted to the light and she quit craning her neck to look toward the front door, she looked directly at us and recoiled. She tried to lower the blind, but it took her a few seconds to figure it out. She yanked at the cord and finally gave up, turning and lurching from the room.

We had scared her, and I felt terrible as we dashed back to my house. The other guys, except for Tom, were giggling and laughing, talking about how witchlike she looked. It was time for a meeting in the coal bin to talk about it.

Jon and Dan and Joel looked puzzled as it became obvious that Tom and I were no longer having any fun with this.

"It's obvious she's not a witch," I said.

"Looked to me like she *was*," Jon said, and the other two laughed.

"I'm serious," I said. "This is a lonely, scared old woman who keeps up her yard and her garden and her house. That's no witch. And we all know full well there are no bodies buried in that house. Tom and I have been researching this, and we've figured out what happened to every member of that family except Mrs. Butchbaker's daughter—Pamela—who went to high school with my parents."

"This is no fun," Joel said slowly.

"Of course it's not," Tom said. "What's the fun in hassling somebody, especially somebody who doesn't deserve it?"

"Well, she chases off people and animals," Dan said.

"So what? So would you if they were bothering you. That doesn't make her a monster or even mean. Everybody who's come onto that property except the grocery boy has been there to make her life miserable. We shouldn't have anything to do with that. That's not what we're about."

"What *are* we about?" Jon asked. "We're supposed to be investigatin' her, so what are we finding?"

"We're all going to get involved in that," I said. "Tom and I have found lots of stuff, and we've copied it so you can read what we've already seen. And we know where to find the rest. This is a woman with an interesting past. We just can't figure out why she all of a sudden stopped living out in the open like everyone else."

"Sounds like schoolwork," Joel called out.

"A little," I said. "But it's fun and interesting, and if you listen to my dad, he says most detective work is just like this. In real life it's not all action and fast cars and shooting. It's looking up stuff and fitting clues together and making sense of everything."

"Well," Jon said, "what have you found?"

Tom and I told them all about the Haases moving here from Germany by way of South America.

"South America!?" Jon said. "Isn't that where the Nazi war criminals escaped to after the Nuremberg trials?"

Tom and I looked at each other. "You know about this stuff?" I asked.

"Sure!" Jon said. "We studied this at our school. The Nuremberg trials were where they sentenced all the Nazi leaders that killed so many Jews. The ones who got away escaped to South America, and a lot of them still live there. People are catching them all the time."

"You think Mrs. Butchbaker's husband was a Nazi?" Joel said.

"Not her husband," Tom said. "More likely her father. But we're going to have to keep digging to find out what he was. Toby and I had it narrowed down to him being a Nazi, or a Jew, or someone who protected Jews during the war. But he was in South America long before the Nuremberg trials."

"That means he knew he had to get out before that," Jon said. "Don't you think?"

"Maybe. But we'd better not jump to any conclusions."

"What's all this stuff about?" Joel asked. "Nazis and Jews and war crimes?"

"You've got a lot to learn," I said.

"Yeah, but it sounds cool. Count me in."

"We'll count you in," Tom said, "but you probably won't think it's so cool when you find out what the Nazis did to the Jews."

"What are Jews anyway?" Joel said.

"You *do* have a lot to learn," Tom said.

"Well, I know Jesus and the disciples were Jews, but I don't think I know any Jews."

"I don't know *what* to think," I said. "We just have to keep reading. When they moved in here, someone thought they were Jews or Nazis, one or the other. Or maybe they just hated them because they were foreigners, speaking another language."

"Yeah," Tom said. "And for sure the wrong language for that time in history."

"I've got to talk with Mrs. Lawrence again at seven," I said. "Is the newspaper office still open?"

"No," Tom said. "But the library is open till nine."

"Let's go!" Dan and Jon said.

Joel added, "I'm in!"

On our way out the door my mother said, "Where are you guys going?"

I knew she wouldn't believe us, but I told her anyway.

"Right," she said. "The library. And I'm the Easter Bunny."

Puzzle Pieces

It was fun to see the rest of the guys get as excited about history as Tom and I had become. They were actually quiet, looking up stuff, comparing notes, finding books. I had to leave at about quarter to seven to get to Mrs. Lawrence's, and the guys were still working away. We agreed to meet back at my house later that evening. The week was moving fast and getting away from us, but now we were finally doing something meaningful and fun.

Mrs. Lawrence had changed. She was no longer playing games with me, making me guess things. She still wanted me to learn on my own, but she was part of it now. She was interested and intrigued herself.

"You know, it's been years since I've been allowed to care about Star Butchbaker."

"Allowed?" I said.

"Star wouldn't let anyone into her life. I tried to keep in touch with her, but I got married, raised a family here, and had to keep up with her by letters."

"You lived this close, and you had to *write?* Couldn't you call her or go see her?"

"No. She made it clear that John didn't want that, and I didn't want to make things difficult for her. I got the message that she wasn't happy. John was—abusive. You know what that means?"

I shrugged. "Sort of."

"I don't know if he hit her or hurt her, but he was a drinker, so it wouldn't surprise me. The only thing she would admit to me was that he screamed at her and criticized her all the time. She couldn't do anything right. Then all of a sudden her letters stopped. I feared that he had found one of them and punished her for telling me too much."

Mrs. Lawrence managed to rise from her chair and move slowly to the kitchen. "You want anything?" she asked.

"Already ate, thank you," I said.

"A polite boy," she said absently. "Don't see too many of those these days. I'm getting myself a cookie and some tea. You're sure you don't want any?"

"I'm sure."

"You're going to want one when you smell mine, and I won't be sharing," she said.

I loved when she tried to act gruff like that. It was just her way of trying to persuade me to order a cookie while she was up and getting them.

"That's all right," I said, smiling. "I'll wait until you're all settled back in your chair before deciding to let you get me one."

She laughed. "You'll be getting it yourself then. I have to combine my errands and do them all at once. No wasted time or movement, you understand. Now let me get on with my story before you have to leave."

"Yes, ma'am."

She sat back down with her tea and cookie. "One of the last letters I got from Star said that she had a baby girl. Pamela."

"My parents went to high school with her."

"Did they? And did she speak English?"

"They said something about her having a very thick accent."

"And yet she was born in the States. Star told me that John insisted they speak only German at home, same as they had done in her home, except when they were waiting on the customers at the five-and-dime. I don't know how Friedrich Haase or John Butchbaker got along, speaking only in German most of the day."

"What did John Butchbaker do for a living?"

"He was an auto mechanic when he was working. But he didn't work much or often. Always on the sauce."

"The sauce?"

"Booze, liquor, beer, wine, you name it. John Butchbaker never saw a bottle he didn't like. I knew that about him before Star did."

"You knew her husband before she did?"

"He tried to date me."

I couldn't believe how the news just kept dropping out of Mrs. Lawrence's mouth, drip by drip. "Where did you meet him?"

"Well, it's kind of a long story. Our business college was located on the top two floors of a bank building in downtown Kalamazoo. John was the custodian for the bank, and they were apparently the landlords for the college too, because he also did janitorial work up there. When he was sober, he was charming, I'll give him that."

"Did you understand German?"

"Only the most rudimentary terms. But he knew enough English and knew he would have to speak some to get next to any of the women at the business college. He was about my age and Star's, and most of the girls were younger. Many of them had their eyes on him, but he was interested only in Star. At least it seemed that way to me."

"But he tried to date you?"

"Only to make Star jealous, I'm sure. He talked to her, looked at her, teased her, flirted with her, and asked her out every day. She didn't turn him down. She just smiled and ignored him. When he did finally get her to say something, she spoke in German, and he lit up. They'd begin jabbering to each other in German, and no one knew what they were saying."

"So she fell in love with him?"

"I don't think so. That's what made it so sad. He used to pull me aside and ask me for advice on how to get through to her that he really cared about her. I told him to just tell her. He complained that she just wouldn't go out with him. I told him that was *his* problem, but then he asked if *I* would go out with him to get her attention. Pardon me, but I told him to drop dead."

"You did?"

"'Drop dead?' he says. 'Wouldn't you feel bad if I did just that?' And I told him, 'You ask me to go out just to make another girl jealous? You're lucky *I* don't make you drop dead.' 'You wouldn't kill me,' he says. 'I'm in love with your best friend.' I told him, 'She's not my best friend, and anyway you can't be in love with somebody you hardly know.' 'I know her well enough,' he says. And I tell him, 'And I know her well enough to know she's not going to be interested in a guy who always has liquor on his breath.'"

"You actually said that to him?"

"I did. And in those words, if my old memory's working at all. I was pretty direct in those days."

"You're pretty direct these days," I said, and she laughed.

"The point is, Tobin, I didn't know Star well, but I felt sorry for her. She was living in this big house with a wealthy, foreign father and a quiet, stoic mother and a brother and a bunch of sisters—all of whom have died by now, by the way. You'll find their obituaries in those papers you're studying if you look far enough."

"Was she any good in school?"

"Not bad for a girl whose first language was German. It was very, very difficult for her. The language, the interacting with people—very painful. She was so shy."

"What did John Butchbaker say when you accused him of being a drunk?"

"Well, I didn't actually say he was a drunk, but that's what I feared. And eventually he did become an alcoholic—if he wasn't one when she met him."

"How did he ever get her to marry him?"

Mrs. Lawrence looked at the clock. I hated when she did that. But she must have figured she had enough time to tell me, because she started in on the story. "He kept badgering me to go out. I kept turning him down. Finally he said, 'What if I told you that I don't like Star anymore but I really, really like you now?'

"I told him, 'I'd say you're the lying scoundrel I always thought you were.' He says, 'You're jealous! I knew it! You've always had a thing for me, and you're just mad because I'd rather be going out with Star!' I said, 'Dream on,' or some such. I wanted a boyfriend, sure. We all did. I looked forward to getting married like most people did. But I certainly wasn't interested in John Butchbaker. Besides the fact that he had no real prospects in life, he just wasn't my type. I wanted someone serious and dependable, maybe a little shy. He saw himself as a lady's man."

"Is that why Star wasn't interested?"

"Actually, Star *was* interested. She would often tell me on our bus rides home that she wished she knew how to say yes to him. I told her, 'You agree to go out with him, you'll wind up marrying him, sure as I'm sitting here.' I was right too. She laughed me off, but I was right."

"Did he finally give up on you?"

"No, he was sure the only way to get to her was through me, so he kept up the charm. I was never really mean to him.

I always smiled when I told him the truth. I didn't want to embarrass him. I would have been just as considerate of an American boy, but a German—a European of any type—I knew enough to be careful with. It was a fact that those men had fragile egos. It was simply not part of their culture to be set straight or put in their place by a woman. So I was careful. But he knew where I stood."

"I still don't know how he ever got Star to go out with him."

"I had a little to do with that, I'm sorry to say. I kept telling her she was too good for him. I told him the same thing, which made him only want her all the more. But it was obvious to me that she was intrigued by him and wanted to have the courage to go out with him. That led to one of the few real personal conversations we ever had.

"She told me that she needed some break from the suffocating house she was living in. Her father ruled with an iron fist, made everyone speak German, eat German, read German. She said it was as if they still lived in Germany, plopped right in the middle of America."

"Mrs. Lawrence, were they Jews?"

"What do you think?" she asked. "After all your study, what do you think?"

"I think they weren't."

"You are correct."

"Then were they Nazis?"

"What do you think?"

"I hope not."

"I hope not too," she said.

"You don't know?"

"I know."

"But you're still not going to tell me."

"You have to study and research, Tobin."

"I *am!*"

"Then you should be able to put the dates and the facts together and decide for yourself what role Friedrich Haase played in Germany. Why did they come to the United States by way of South America?"

"A lot of Nuremberg war criminals did that."

"Haase was long gone before the Nuremberg trials," she said.

"I know."

"Then that should tell you something."

"Maybe he knew he would be found guilty and thought he had to escape first."

"Maybe. Except for one glaring thing."

"I'm missing it."

"You want me to give you this big a clue?"

"Yes!"

"You're sure?"

"Please!"

"He never changed his name."

"Ma'am?"

"He never changed his name. Read your newspaper accounts, follow the story. The Haase family moved from Germany to South America and then to Michigan on legal passports and visas bearing their original names. They were the Haases when they lived in Germany. They were the Haases when they lived in South America. They were the Haases when they moved here. Star was a Haase when I met her and a Haase until she married John Butchbaker. Now she's a Butchbaker, though he's long dead, and I'll bet she wishes she were still a Haase."

"Thanks for the big clue," I said. "I guess I can assume the Haases weren't running away, because using their own names would make them easy to find. I know they're still finding old Nazi war criminals all over the world even now."

"Very good."

"But somehow you got me off the track of why Star Haase ever married John Butchbaker."

"Don't blame that on me, Tobin. I'm an old lady. You want me to stay on the track, you've got to keep me there."

Starting to Wish

As I sat staring at Mrs. Lawrence, I began to long for the opportunity to talk with Mrs. Butchbaker. I never would have guessed I would even dream of such a thing. Now it seemed important to me. I felt sorry for her for some reason. I knew a lot more about her than I had ever known before, but still it seemed I didn't know her at all.

"You've got to tell me how those two ever got married," I pleaded.

Mrs. Lawrence sighed and looked at the clock. "This story is going to take longer than I've got," she said. "I'll start it, but you'll have to come back."

"May I?"

"May you? Of course you may! This is the most fun I've had in years! My son checks in on me every day, you know, but there's nothing more for us to talk about. He's a good boy with a family he's already raised and a wife who demands a lot. She's all right. I mean, I guess I'd be jealous of a mother who required this much upkeep too, but DeWayne is not the type to sit and gossip."

"Are we gossiping?" I asked, and I must have looked alarmed.

"I don't think so," she said. "I'm certainly not saying anything I wouldn't say to Star's face. And if it keeps you kids from thinking she's a witch . . . well, what's wrong with that?"

"I wouldn't want to be gossiping about her," I said. "I mean, I guess maybe I might want to, but I know I shouldn't!"

That made Mrs. Lawrence roar. She laughed so hard she began to cough, spill her tea, and almost drop her cookie plate. I stood to help her, but she waved me off. "Polite *and* honest!" she said. "What planet are you from? Gossip *is* fun! But that's not what this is. You worried she was a witch, and then you worried the family were Nazis. Now you're a little sympathetic, I can tell. We're not doing her any harm."

"How long has it been since you've talked to her?" I asked, hoping Mrs. Lawrence might feel the way I did—that it would be fun to break through to Mrs. Butchbaker one of these days.

"How long? Oh, my. Probably more than twenty years ago and—of all places—on the bus again. I saw her sitting there, looking out the window. I immediately went and sat next to her. I knew she knew someone had sat next to her, but she didn't turn. At first I thought she didn't realize it was me. I said, 'Well, doesn't this bring back memories?' She said— without turning to face me—'It certainly does, Victoria.'"

"Your first name is Victoria? I don't think I knew that."

"You didn't? Why do you think DeWayne calls me Queenie?"

"I didn't know he did."

"You *are* young, aren't you? For many years everybody in this neighborhood knew who Queenie was. Even those bootleggers who once lived in your house. They didn't mess with me, let me tell you. Anyway, back to my story. I asked Star if she had ever done anything with her business college education. She said no and asked if I had. I told her I worked at the bank in the same building as the college for a few years while my kids were growing up. She said she had an account at that bank and never knew I worked there."

"And . . ."

"And that was it. I asked her how John and Pamela were, and she just nodded and kept looking out the window. I told her it was OK if she didn't want to talk, and she said thank you and didn't talk. I asked her if it would be all right if I called on her one day. She said nothing. I wrote her notes a few times after that. Called her a few times. He answered and said she wasn't available. I asked once if I could leave my number. He said he didn't have anything to write with and asked if I would just call back. Once I said, 'John, you know me. Will you tell her I called?' He hung up on me. It was as if he was no more thrilled with the marriage than she was, and they both blamed me. God forgive me, but except for an annual Christmas card, I gave up."

"And you never heard from her."

"Not a word. Not a call. Not a note. Nothing."

"That's weird."

"It sure is. Well, now, I shouldn't have said 'nothing.' She showed up at the viewing when my husband passed away."

"She did?"

"I saw her from across the room. And she did sign the visitors' book. In that beautiful handwriting she signed 'Mr. and Mrs. John Butchbaker.' I don't know why she did that, because no one saw him there. By then I believe he had left her. We sent her a note, thanking her for her kindness, but we never heard from her again."

"How do people like that ever get together in the first place?"

"That still bothers you, doesn't it, Tobin?"

"It seems like there'd be less bad marriages if people knew better than to get married in the first place."

"That's what I tried to tell her. Then she asks me to stand up for her and be a witness."

"Back up."

"All right. Finally, after being pressured by him every day to either go out with him or talk *her* into going out with him, I gave in."

"You went out with him?"

"No! Never! But she was pining away on the bus about how she really would like to get to know him better—and he was German after all, and they could communicate. I told her to get on the stick."

"What does that mean?"

"I told her to just accept his invitation and find out for herself that he's an undependable drinker and get him out of her system. How was I to know she had never dated anyone before and would be swept off her feet?"

"He turned on the charm?"

"That's putting it mildly. The only problem was, even though she was in her mid-twenties by then, they had to meet in secret."

"I'll bet her family was against it."

"Her father was. She even told him John was German, but that didn't make any difference at first. I had to help them set up the date."

"Why?"

"Because she could never muster the courage to say yes. I didn't really want her to go out with him, but I was tired of hearing about it. I knew she wanted to and that she would always wonder if she should have. Anyway, I was convinced that if she spent much time with him alone, she'd come to her senses. A guy like that doesn't wear well when he has to behave for a few hours at a time."

"So how'd you get them together?"

"You make it sound like it was all my doing. It wasn't. I played a part, sure. He told me he was going to ask her to go roller-skating. I said I didn't know if she roller-skated. He said he didn't care. He asked her, and she didn't answer or she evaded the question. But on the way home on the bus it was all she could talk about.

"'So you're going?' I asked. 'Oh, no,' she said, 'I wouldn't know how to accept.' I said, 'How about just saying yes?' She shook her head."

"So how did you make it happen?"

"I'm getting to that. I asked her, 'If I was to tell him that you'd meet him there, would you do it?' She says, 'I might.' I said, 'Do you need me to go along with you?' And she says, 'I might.' I said, 'And would you like me to disappear when he gets there?' And she says, 'I might.'"

"So they met at a roller rink?"

"I told him she would meet him there, and he just about died. He tried to hug me. I wouldn't let him. He jumped around and whooped and hollered. I told her she would have to be there by eight, and she reminded me that I had promised to go with her. I didn't really want to, but I did.

"I don't know what story she told her parents—probably something about going out with me. She was dressed kind of plain—plainer than I was certainly—not the way I would have dressed if I was trying to impress a man. He showed up sober and looking sharp, all smiles and smooth. I drifted away and then left, worrying about her all night. I wished she would have called or somehow let me know she got home all right.

"The next morning she thanked me a hundred times for setting it up. Now she looked radiant, dressing as if for him. It was as if I didn't exist when she floated past him in the hall and waved that little wave. He smiled and blushed. She was smitten. He didn't have much more to say to me after that. He had what he wanted, and she thought she was in love with him."

"How did her dad take it?"

"I suppose he got used to the idea. She introduced him to her family, and they were so thrilled he was German that they welcomed him in. One thing her father insisted on was that if they got married, they would live with the family."

"Did John and Star want that?"

"That's the way it was done back then. It was the most economical. In that house, it was a good thing her fiancé was German, because no English was spoken there. I felt a little left out because, though she talked to me on the way to and from work every day, it was all about her and John, John and her, them and the family, the family and them. I was flattered to be asked to stand up for her and agreed to do it, even hoping and praying I had been wrong about him.

"I didn't smell alcohol on him like I had before, so I thought maybe she was the best thing that had ever happened to him. I thought I had misjudged him. We all make mistakes in judgment. But it wasn't long before I knew my mistake had been doubting my first impression."

"What happened?"

"They were married and moved in with her family. Almost from the beginning, John and her father were squabbling with each other. Shouting matches, even fistfights, were commonly known in the neighborhood. Friedrich would kick John out, Star would threaten to go with him, Friedrich would forbid that, John would beg forgiveness and make promises, and all would be well again for a month or two. Meanwhile, Star was no longer talking to me."

"Why? Did she blame you?"

"I don't really think so. I think she was disappointed, humiliated, and didn't want to admit she'd made the biggest mistake of her life. Here she thought this charming German would rescue her from her family, and he simply became part of it."

"And she didn't want you to know?"

"She knew I knew. That was the problem. John quickly went back to his old drinking ways. Meanwhile, her father was getting older and was not well. He eventually killed himself."

"He did?"

"And that made everybody think he had been a Nazi criminal, that he had tortured and sentenced to death and killed Jews in concentration camps."

"Did he? Is that what we're going to find in the old newspapers?"

"What do you think?"

"I think not, because then he would have changed his name and tried to hide out."

"Right, so people weren't thinking clearly when they assumed his suicide was from guilt over war crimes, were they?"

I shook my head. "Why did he do it then?"

"The answer to that will tell you what you need to know about Star Butchbaker."

"So tell me."

Mrs. Lawrence wagged a bony finger at me. "Oh, no," she said. "You've done so well up to now. It's time for you to keep digging. And it's time for my program."

"But—"

"Run along now, Tobin, so you don't outstay your welcome."

This was fun but frustrating, and I wanted more than ever to someday sit and talk like this with Mrs. Butchbaker. At the very least she'd had a tough life. But I wanted to know more. What would make her so bitter, so cold, so angry that she would shut out of her life even those like Mrs. Lawrence who cared about her?

I didn't expect the answers to come from anywhere but Mrs. Lawrence or Mrs. Butchbaker herself. But when the guys got back from the library, they had more information than I ever dreamed they would find. I would not lose my desire to talk with Mrs. Butchbaker, but I would have a lot more to go on with what they brought home.

Getting Warmer

W ait till you see what we found!" Red Jon said as the guys bounded into the old coal bin.

"I don't want to wait!" I said.

"We think Friedrich Haase might have been a Nazi!"

"I don't," I said.

"You don't know what we turned up."

"But I have good reason to believe that he wasn't a Nazi."

"Slow down there, Toby," Tom said. "The evidence is pretty strong."

"So's mine," I said. "Unless you can prove he changed his name."

"I hope he didn't," Tom said. "It was through his name that we traced his papers all the way from Kalamazoo to Argentina to Munich. It's Friedrich Haase, all right, and we think he was a member of Hitler's staff."

"Show me," I said.

"Well, we're going to have to prove this by checking his records at the county courthouse," Tom said, "but the librarian thinks that should be no problem. She says the Freedom of Information Act allows the public to see those things. We can check it out when they open in the morning."

"What are you going to check?"

"The stuff in the library shows when Haase came from Germany, when he got to Argentina, and when he came to the United States. There's a picture of him in the paper from his passport photo, and it shows him wearing the cap the leaders of the German military wore during the time of Hitler. That's probably why his house was vandalized and people kept hassling the family for years."

"That went on for *years?*" I repeated.

Tom spread out some copies he'd made of old newspapers. "Look," he said.

It hadn't been just while the house was being built that swastikas were drawn on it. Once the house was finished, someone had painted on the garage, "Nazis burn. Nazis go home. Nazis die."

"Did you know," Tom asked, "that their house was actually burned to the ground once?"

"Mrs. Lawrence didn't tell me that. I wonder if she knows."

"She had to know," Red Jon said. "Maybe she forgot."

"Maybe she chose to forget," Tom said. "Mrs. Butchbaker lost a little sister in that fire, and her father felt responsible. In his suicide note he said he had brought this on his own flesh and blood because of his past."

I sat down and shook my head. "But the Haases traveled under their own names and never tried to hide. Why? Doesn't that say they *weren't* Nazis? Wouldn't they try to disappear if Friedrich Haase had been a Nazi criminal? And how do the dates on his passport line up with the concentration camps and all that?"

"That's something we'll have to check out in the morning," Tom said. "But you make a good point about their name. It doesn't make sense."

"It wasn't *my* point. It was Mrs. Lawrence's."

Thursday morning I made the mistake of going to the county courthouse downtown and asking for the Friedrich Haase records. Only Red Jon was with me, so we must have looked too young.

We sent Old Tom back, and he said, "Sorry I sent those kids for those records. They're for me."

"Well, sir, in the future you should always get them for yourself."

"I will. Sorry."

And he was given a huge file folder for which we had to pay only the copying fee. We ran to the library to check out the stuff.

Everything was in that file, from the amount of money the Haases paid for the land where they built their house, to the insurance payment they received when it burned, to the birth dates of their children, you name it.

"Toby is right," Tom said as we pored over the documents. "Something doesn't add up. This is not a guy who's running from anything or anyone. He's living right out in the open in America. Easy to find. The vandals who burned his house thought he was guilty of something, but the government didn't, or they would have arrested him."

We found evidence that he had been a huge lumberman in Germany, that his business faltered some in Argentina, and so he went into the banking and retail business. By the time he bought the five-and-dime in Kalamazoo, he had been able to get his business dollars released from Germany and wired to him. He was a very wealthy man.

"When did he leave Germany?" I asked.

The guys sifted through the papers trying to find it. The Haases' entry papers into Argentina were issued in January

75

1938. That was before Germany started invading the rest of Europe and before most of the concentration camp deaths.

"He was not an old man then," I said. "Why did he leave the Nazi military? Or was he booted out?"

"If he was booted out, why did he still wear the hat?" Tom asked. "And why was he booted?"

"You know what Mrs. Lawrence would say," I said.

"We know," Red Jon said. "More study."

We went back to the library and pulled down gigantic volumes of World War Two reference books. One was totally in German and listed the Nazi military regime.

"Haase has to be spelled the same way in German," Tom said. "Look in there."

A couple of us spent the next few hours looking. Finally, in a listing of the officers in the National Socialist Party military for the early 1930s, we found several Friedrich Haases. How could we tell which one was he? We cross-checked his birth date with the date on his passport and visa, and, sure enough, there was one exact duplicate.

I felt like an archaeologist. It was one thing to find a local guy listed in the county courthouse file of records, but to find him in a German reference book from the 1930s,—now that was really something! We carefully noted his rank and serial number and kept looking in later volumes to see how high he rose in the military.

By late 1936 he was in the German high command, a Nazi military leader who would have had to have been one of Hitler's top men. Was it possible? Had we traced a Nazi war criminal? But why was he never hunted down? Why was he never brought to justice? Vandals thought they were onto him and tried to punish him by terrorizing his family, but could he have really been guilty and not tried to hide?

We kept digging. At last we found it. In a roster of German high command military personnel in 1938, Friedrich Haase was no longer listed. Several of his compatriots were no longer listed either. Had he quit the military? Had he been discharged? There was no record of that.

Friday morning we dug through the library again, making scrapbooks of copies of local newspaper clippings about the Haase and Butchbaker families. We were going to get to the bottom of this once and for all. We had begun by wanting to find out if Mrs. Butchbaker was a witch. Now we wanted to find out who she really was.

It seemed to me that we had sort of adopted her. She'd become someone we didn't know but wanted to know. We knew a lot about her, at least about her family. And I wasn't the only one who wanted to talk to her. By the time we were this deep into the research, we all did.

"This woman needs to know somebody cares about her," Red Jon said.

We all looked at him.

"I was thinking the same thing," Tom said. "Something in her past—maybe a lot of stuff—makes her the way she is today. Wow! Oh, man, look at this!"

He was looking at a family picture of the Haases just after John Butchbaker joined their family.

"Is that her?" Big Dan asked. "She's beautiful!"

She was. Star Haase Butchbaker was wearing a frilly, lacy, white dress and standing shyly with her arm through her husband's arm. He looked like a city slicker with oily hair combed straight back and a pencil-thin mustache, wire-rimmed glasses, and a baggy suit.

The guys all gathered around to stare at the photo.

"More than age has made her ugly now," Jon said. "She hardly looks like the same person at all."

"It's her, though," Tom said. "Look at the ear—and the hand."

They were similar to her present-day photos. But the rest of her look now was haggard and wary and suspicious. Ugly. It was sad what the years and the memories had done to her.

I spent late Friday afternoon with Mrs. Lawrence again, telling her what we'd come up with.

"You're close," she said. "I'm going to let you discover the rest for yourself."

"You knew her father was a member of the German high command and left that to emigrate to Argentina?" I asked.

"Of course I knew. And now you know without my telling you. Just don't forget that he didn't steal away in the night under a phony name. He had a valid passport and visa and took his entire family aboard ship in broad daylight."

"But why? If he had been in trouble with Hitler, he never would have got out of the country, right?"

"It would seem so. There is an answer, Tobin, and it is in the history books you boys are going through now. Mr. Haase was a decorated military officer. And then he was not. But he was not punished or tried or discharged. What happened?"

"No hints?"

"You don't need any hints. The answer is there. You find it."

I had never known detective work could be so much fun. I always wished it was as dramatic and exciting as TV shows made it look. But my dad had always said it was hard work with occasional victories. We had discovered a lot and learned a lot, but we still had to figure this one out.

Friday night we fell asleep earlier than usual, worried that the week was fast coming to a close. We wanted to sort this thing out and see if we could actually talk to Mrs. Butchbaker someday.

I woke up at midnight, thinking. That hadn't happened to me since I was a kid and Dad was away on a trip. I'd waked up worried and wakened my mother. She had prayed with me and assured me that God was watching over Dad and would bring him back.

I couldn't wake her up now, not for this. But something was nagging at me. The answer had to be in the printouts and photocopies we had made. There was hardly anything we had missed.

Everything was in a big stack on the desk in the spare bedroom, where Dan and Joel had decided to sleep that night.

I tiptoed in there and found them sound asleep. Jon and Tom were dead to the world in my room. I gathered up all the stuff and lugged it down to the kitchen table. No one was around, and I didn't feel tired.

I kept trying to sort it out. I didn't know what difference it made in Star Haase's life—the woman who had become Mrs. Butchbaker. But Mrs. Lawrence seemed to think it was important: whatever had taken the Haases from Germany to the United States, after a few years in Argentina, had to be significant.

In the wee hours of the morning, I was reading a history of Adolf Hitler himself. I read and read and read. It was not written for someone my age, and I had to read it over and over to figure out what it meant. I even used a dictionary, and that helped a little. Finally I put it all together.

In the early 1930s, Hitler started planning for war. He had promised all along that he was for peace. But his book, *Mein Kampf,* made clear he eventually wanted to take over all of Europe.

In 1935 he announced that Germany was rearming, getting more weapons, which violated the Versailles Treaty the Germans had signed.

He made pacts with Rome and Japan and then met secretly with his top military leaders in November 1937. There Hitler outlined his war plans. I knew I was onto something now. Friedrich Haase was still in the German military high command at that time. He would have been in on that meeting.

And here came the missing piece of the puzzle. One of the books said, "Several of his top military leaders objected and were dismissed."

But Friedrich Haase had not been dismissed. He seemed to simply disappear. He left the country with his family but was not in hiding. Was it possible he was one of those who disagreed with Hitler but didn't say so? Maybe he left Germany as if on some sort of business, then retired from the military without making any comment on Hitler's plans?

That would make him a hero in one sense, a person who would not agree with a dictator's plans for an illegal war. But it would also make him a coward, one who might feel responsible for all that happened after that, because he had not stood in disagreement with Hitler. Millions of Jews were killed, and the German invasions of other European countries caused all sorts of death.

I believed I had discovered who Friedrich Haase really was: a man who knew when something was wrong but a man who didn't have the courage to do what was right. No wonder he became a miserable person and made everyone around him the same.

Mrs. Lawrence Drops the Other Shoe

Old Victoria Lawrence was waiting by the door when I showed up Saturday morning. "I'm starting to practice," she said. "I want to get in shape."

"In shape for what?" I said, moving past her and into a chair near hers in front of the TV. She used a walker to get back across the room and sit down. I had seen the walker before, but I had never seen her use it.

"One of these days, and sooner than I ever thought, I'm going to walk to Star Butchbaker's myself. I don't care how long it takes me or what kind of a wrap I need to wear. I know it's summer and all, but I may need a shawl for all I know. But I won't accept a ride, and my son would probably scold me if he knew, but I'm walking down there anyway. I'll force her hand. Fifty years is plenty long enough to let her shut me out of her life. And Tobin, I have you to thank for reawakening me to her. Not that I haven't thought about her many times . . ."

"What if she won't see you?"

"She'll see me. And she'll know I walked down there by myself and that I won't leave until she invites me in. I'll camp out on her porch if I have to."

"I'd sure like to go with you."

"Of course, you'll go with me. Who else would go?"

"Your son?"

"My son wants nothing to do with that house. He was accused of burning it down once. He was innocent and finally proved it, but he's never forgotten that."

"So you *did* know the place had been burned to the ground."

"Of course, I knew. Anyone who lived in Kalamazoo back then knew. That was when it came out—all of Friedrich Haase's background, I mean."

"Everybody found out he had been one of Hitler's military leaders?"

The old woman nodded. "They wanted to string him up. Some people were sympathetic because one of his daughters died in that fire. He wound up killing himself, he felt so responsible. It was awful."

"I don't get it," I said. I told her what I had discovered about Hitler's secret meeting with his military leaders in November 1937. "Mr. Haase must have disagreed with Hitler, and that's why he left. What could he have done to stop what happened over there?"

Mrs. Lawrence shook her head. "That's what everybody said, not just about him but about all the people in places of leadership who should have spoken out against Hitler. They all pointed fingers at each other and waited for the other person to do something. Where were the pastors, the priests, the church people? Do you realize that the bravest people were the German citizens and some Dutch and Polish citizens who let Jews hide out in their homes? They risked their lives. In fact, many were caught and sent to prison camps. Many died, just because they dared to harbor Jews from Hitler's troops.

"But there were also Jews who worked *with* Hitler, turning in their friends and neighbors, helping the Nazis carry out their orders. Those people were scared to death, of course, and maybe many of them felt they had no choice. The only way to eat and stay alive and stay off those trains to the camps was to turn in other people. Tobin, there were lots of people who could feel as guilty as Friedrich Haase."

I sat there feeling old. No wonder adults didn't much like to talk about this stuff. It was no fun. It was awful. "My friends found an article that told about Mr. Haase's suicide note. He said he felt responsible for what had happened to his home and his daughter because of his past."

"Yes, and frankly that didn't help much. That was what started changing everything for Star Butchbaker. She'd had a tough enough life as it was, trying to live under the rule of her father. He had become an embittered man, and though he had built that big lumber business even while serving in the military in Germany, it seemed he took no sense of pride in his business anymore."

I pulled my chair to where I could look right at Mrs. Lawrence when she spoke. She had grown quieter and was more difficult to hear. But I wanted to catch everything. She was no longer making it hard for me to figure things out. It was as if she was now rewarding me for having worked so hard, researched and studied and read so much.

Mrs. Lawrence stared at the wall and spoke as if I weren't there. "Star's marriage to John Butchbaker was doomed from the start. They put on a good front at the wedding. It wasn't big, but it was held at the house, the first and last time I was ever in there. The whole family was there, of course, and a few—just a very few—of Mr. Haase's business associates and their wives. The wedding was a very embarrassing, awkward thing. I hated it."

"Why?"

"Mr. Haase insisted that it be conducted entirely in German. I caught only a little of it, and while the family and the bride and groom understood everything, the guests were not happy. That was plain. Star seemed upset with her father, who was stony. And I could tell that whatever chemistry had existed between Star and John was already gone."

"Already? By the day of their wedding?"

She nodded. "They whispered to each other in German the whole time, so I didn't know what they were saying. But it was obvious neither was happy. Star seemed embarrassed and angry with her father, but she didn't dare confront him, I suppose, especially in front of other people. John kept scolding her, whispering, but always in her face or close to her ear. She seemed to be pulling away."

"The whole ceremony was in German, huh?"

"And the worst part was an embarrassing little episode that could have otherwise been very charming. I understood a lot of the wedding ceremony because I knew what was going on. But after that, Mr. Haase told his wife—in German, of course—to take the guests on a tour of the house. I knew this only because Star whispered to me what he'd said."

"So you got to see the whole mansion?"

She nodded again. "It was, and I assume still is, magnificent. But this was a terrible ordeal. All the family members and the few guests traipsed up the grand oak staircase and saw the immaculate home. It was something they were proud of and rightfully so. We were shown the newlyweds' new quarters, just a small room with a bath down the hall. They looked embarrassed and giggled. But what was so difficult about it was that both the Haases, Mr. and Mrs., continued to speak only in German throughout the tour. If I hadn't known a smattering of German, I would have been completely lost."

"Weird," I said.

"It was more than weird, Tobin," Mrs. Lawrence said.

"The other couples who had been invited were plainly perturbed, and one of the men spoke up. He said, 'Fred, I can't understand a thing you're saying.' And Mr. Haase loudly corrected him. I couldn't make out all of it, but it was obvious he was telling the man that in his own house he would be referred to as Friedrich.

"Well, the other man would have none of that. He began ranting about 'You conceited Germans' and 'It's no wonder Hitler made a mess of your country,' and things like that. I thought they were going to come to blows."

"Come to blows?"

"Fight. Hit each other."

"Oh."

"But Mr. Haase simply refused to be badgered into speaking English, and the guests began asking for their coats. It was most unpleasant. Friedrich simply led them to a spare bedroom and pointed to where their coats had been piled on a bed. They were to get their own coats and get out was the clear message.

"Well, Mrs. Haase burst into tears and ran down the stairs. Meanwhile, John and Star were arguing loudly in German, and he was squeezing her arm to keep her from dashing away too. I wanted to be anywhere but there, but when I made a move to get my coat, Star looked at me with the most desperate face. I couldn't leave her.

"Mr. Haase bounded down the stairs and grabbed his wife, shouting at her. She immediately joined him at the door, wiped her eyes, and shook hands with those guests who would let her as they left."

"What a way to end a wedding."

"Well, it wasn't over," Mrs. Lawrence said. "They actually served cake and coffee after that to the few of us who remained. No one dared look at either of the Haases. We just sat there eating and drinking and trying to make small talk with each other. Occasionally Mr. Haase would say something in German, and we would nod and smile and pretend to agree. If it seemed he had told a joke or said something funny, we would all nervously chuckle and then turn back to our food. I wished I were dead or at least hidden somewhere."

"That's terrible. I can't imagine how Mrs. Butchbaker must have felt."

"I can," the old woman said. "I remember it like it was yesterday, and it's been half a century ago. It was as if someone had pulled her plug. Her lights went out. Even her fake smile was gone. She ignored her brand-new husband, who sat with his nose in her face, trying desperately to tell her something. She just stared straight ahead. Her father spoke sharply to her once, as if to snap her out of whatever mood she was in. But she wasn't listening to him either.

"I thought maybe Star would break down crying, as her mother had done, but it was as if she had decided to not give anyone the satisfaction of seeing that either. I don't know if she was above all this or merely wanted to appear so, but she had apparently decided not to let any of it get to her."

I shook my head. "The whole thing sounds like a horrible movie."

"That's a perfect description, but it gets worse still. When it finally was time for us to leave, Star embraced me at the door. We had never so much as touched each other before. She was just not that type. Very reserved, very formal. We didn't lean on each other when we sat together on the bus. She had her space, and I had mine. But now she hugged me tight and whispered into my ear—thankfully, in English—'It's been nice knowing you, Victoria.'"

"As if she was not going to see you again?"

"Exactly. I said, 'Star, don't be silly. You'll always be my friend.'

"'No,' she said. 'No, I will not. Just think of me now and again.'

"Tobin, that conversation has stayed with me all these years."

"And you never saw her again?"

"Of course, I saw her. She finished at the business college in another month or so, as I recall. We greeted each other on the bus, and sometimes I even sat with her. She was cordial. She would answer social questions. How are you? How's the family? That kind of a thing. But she always just said everything was fine. Our relationship had changed. I always suspected that John was possessive and didn't want her talking with anyone else, man or woman. I don't recall ever getting a significant word out of her again.

"When she left the business college, she never put her education to work. I noticed she was pregnant and commented on it once, but she didn't respond. When Pamela was born, coming onto forty years ago, I sent her a card and a little gift. I never got an acknowledgment."

"I don't understand this story at all," I said. "I can see she had a rough life. Moving, her father a Nazi and then quitting, making them speak German at home, marrying an alcoholic, having her house burn down, her father committing suicide, losing the rest of her family and her husband. But why did she run from *you?*"

"Why did she run from everybody?" Mrs. Lawrence said. "As far as I know, she hasn't a friend in the world. And who knows whatever happened to her daughter, Pamela?"

Planning the Meeting

W e knew if it was going to happen, it had to happen that night. All the guys agreed that someone had to make a personal contact with Mrs. Butchbaker. Everyone would be going back home after church the next day, and even though I might be the only one going with Mrs. Lawrence, the rest wanted to be at least at my house when it happened. That way they could get the whole story when I got home.

No one knew, of course, whether Mrs. Butchbaker would even answer the door. We wanted to have enough information in advance so we could use everything we knew to try to persuade her to let in Mrs. Lawrence and me.

"Seems to me the first thing we have to do is to find Pamela Butchbaker," Tom said. "Let me talk to your parents about her. They might tell me more than they would tell you." He ran off to ask my mom and dad what they remembered about her from high school.

The rest of us were reading all the stuff about Hitler and

the Nazis and Mr. Haase. It became clear what had happened. He may have killed himself because his youngest daughter died in a fire, but he had been feeling guilty for years for not having done anything to stop the German invasions and the massacre of millions of Jews.

Tom came back from talking to my parents with the news that neither of them had really known Pamela Butchbaker. Both had known who she was and had been in school with her since elementary days. But the poor girl had suffered because, even though she was born in Kalamazoo, she didn't have a father anyone knew and she spoke with a German accent.

"That never made any sense to your parents," Tom said. "Everybody knew her dad was an alcoholic and that her parents were separated and then divorced. When they were in high school, her father disappeared for a few months and was then found dead somewhere. Pamela Butchbaker was a year behind your parents, but your mom had some vague recollection that she may have been sick most of their senior year— might have missed the last half of that school year, though your dad doesn't remember that. We should check and see if she ever graduated."

So it was back to the library to look up yearbooks. In the two years' worth of volumes when Pamela Butchbaker was a freshman and a sophomore, she was listed and pictured. But for her junior year she was listed as not pictured, though no explanation was given.

In the yearbook for her senior year, Pamela Butchbaker was again listed as not pictured, and there was a note that she had been given a diploma "in absentia." We looked that up.

"Absent," Red Jon said. "She wasn't there for graduation, and it looks like she wasn't there for the year either."

Late that morning I went back to Mrs. Lawrence's. "What happened to Pamela Butchbaker?" I asked.

"I wish I knew," she said.

"You don't remember that she was sick, twenty or so years ago?"

Mrs. Lawrence furrowed her brow, as if trying to remember. "Yes! Wasn't she out of school for a while?"

"Maybe a year and a half," I said.

Mrs. Lawrence nodded. "I want to say cystic fibrosis or something. Something that required that Star be with her all the time, pounding on her back to relieve the fluid buildup in her lungs. Eventually she moved away, and I've never seen her return. And Star never goes anywhere. So as far as I know, they haven't seen each other since."

I presented an idea to Mrs. Lawrence. I told her how we junior deputies had come to feel bad about Mrs. Butchbaker and wanted her to know that her neighbors cared about her. We wanted Mrs. Lawrence to visit her—with me there too—that very afternoon.

Mrs. Lawrence was shaking her head as if it was all too sudden, she wasn't up to it, she would have to prepare, Mrs. Butchbaker would never allow it—and I don't know what other excuse might have been running through her head.

I pleaded with her. "I'll walk with you, or we'll drive you."

"No, I would have to walk," she said. "You would have to somehow get word to Star that I'm coming and that she had mighty well better see me."

"You'll do it?"

"I didn't say that. But I'll think on it."

"What would convince you?"

"I'd have to have a lot to talk about, tell her I know what she's been through. Know that whole history."

"We'll get it to you."

"Most of all, I have to have some update on her daughter. I'd hate to waltz in there asking about a daughter who might have been dead for years."

"I'll see what I can do, Mrs. Lawrence," I said. "And thanks!"

"I haven't agreed to anything yet!" she called as I ran out. "I'm just thinking on it!"

I told the guys we needed to locate Pamela Butchbaker.

"Try the Internet," Big Dan said.

"Where?"

"Out of my way," he said, settling his big frame into the chair in front of my computer. He called up a locator service. "It'll cost you just for connect time," he said. "What do we know about her?"

"We know roughly when she was born. Try like thirty-seven to forty years ago."

Dan was typing in the information, getting the correct spelling, last known address, that kind of stuff.

"How does this work?" I asked.

"They check all kinds of databases—Social Security, disability payments, employers, taxes—those things."

He had entered her name, first and last, and everything else we knew about her, including the name of her high school and the year she graduated. The computer started whirring and clicking, and we could hear the hard drive recording information being downloaded from the Internet server. First, there was a list of several Butchbakers, then broken down by first names. We saw "John," in fact lots of Johns. The one associated with the Butchbaker home on our street was listed as deceased and showed the year he died.

Under a list of his survivors was his wife, Hannalore (Star Dawn) Haase Butchbaker of that same address, and one daughter, Pamela Dawn Butchbaker, also of the same address. It showed her date of birth and indicated she was still alive.

"Current address?" Dan tapped in.

A moment later the answer came. "Same as above."

"What does that mean?" I asked. "She lived with her father till he died and now lives where he lived?"

"I don't think so," Dan said, studying the screen.

"Then what?"

"'Same as above' means the same as the previous entry, which was her mother's address."

"So the last known address for her is her mother's house?"

"The last known address is *the* current address," Dan said.

"Impossible," I said.

"Maybe just old information," Dan said, tapping in. "Confirm?"

The answer came scrolling back. "Social security, disability, and welfare checks delivered to the above named at the address listed below."

The address listed below was the address of Star Butchbaker. If the computer was right, Pamela Butchbaker was alive and living with her mother, just down the street.

We looked at each other, then ran as a group to Mrs. Lawrence's house. I made the guys wait on the porch while I told her they were there and asked if we could all come in.

"If you take it easy on an old woman," she said. "I wouldn't mind getting a look at a bunch of young law enforcement officers."

The guys gathered around her and knelt on the floor in a half circle.

"I don't have anything to offer you," she said.

"We're having lunch at Toby's in a few minutes," Tom said. "We just wanted to tell you what we'd discovered."

Mrs. Lawrence sat there shaking her head as we laid it out for her. "I don't like or understand computers," she said. "Almost seems unnatural that all our business could be that easily seen by everybody—even by kids like you. But I guess in this case it's a blessing, isn't it?"

We didn't know what to say.

"Is that enough information for you, ma'am?" I asked. "Should we tell her you're coming to see her?"

"I'm still thinking about it," she said. "You boys will have to come up with a creative way to make sure she gets the message. If you can do that and I can get these old bones motivated, I just might."

"And I can come with you?" I asked.

"I wouldn't go without you," she said. "Who knows what might be hidden in that house?"

We all looked at her, and she smiled. "I'm not afraid of anything," she said, "but, yes, of course, if I go, you go. But only you."

We wolfed down our lunch, filling in my mother on everything that had happened.

"How are you going to communicate with her?" Mom wanted to know.

"Steve Sakay is the only one I can think of," I said.

"I was thinking the same thing," she said. "Check with him to see if he has a delivery going there, and drop a note in it."

"She didn't respond to your note."

"But she didn't really know me. She's been retreating from the world for decades. Everybody treated her mean, and she became bitter and afraid. But I have to believe she might think twice about Mrs. Lawrence coming to see her. In fact, maybe Mrs. Lawrence should write the note."

I called Steve Sakay.

"I've got a delivery going there Monday morning, as usual," he said.

"Any reason it has to wait that long?"

"I guess not. We'd have to call her and tell her it's coming, though. Wouldn't want to leave it outside without her knowing it was there."

"She has a phone?"

"Sure. For emergencies, I guess. She never calls us, but we can call her just to tell her if we're going to be late or whatever."

"We want to put a nice note in the delivery, Steve," I said. "So let me know if she'll let you deliver this afternoon."

"Why should I tell her I'm doing this?"

"You don't need a reason. Just tell her you'd like to make her Monday delivery at two today. Will she tell you not to?"

"She's never said more than two words to me, Toby. I can't imagine her having a bit of a problem with it."

"Call me before you're ready to deliver. I'll get the note to you."

And back we ran to Mrs. Lawrence's with a pen and paper.

Finally Face to Face

I saw a tiny flash on the horizon and a few clouds forming as we entered Mrs. Lawrence's house. I prayed it wouldn't rain. Surely we'd have to drive her then, and if she wouldn't agree to that, she would put off the visit.

The old woman had not seemed to notice any hint of a storm. She carefully wrote out the note in a slow, labored hand, which had a shaky line but was surprisingly readable.

"What do you think, Tobin?" She handed it to me.

It read: "Star, a young friend and I are coming to see you at five o'clock this afternoon. I will ring once and knock twice, and I will stand on your porch until you let me in. Too many years have passed with our pretending each other does not exist. I need to see you and talk with you, and I won't take no for an answer. Your friend forever, Victoria."

"It would convince me," I said. "But you know her better than I do."

"I wish that were true," Mrs. Lawrence said. "Come get me at four-thirty."

Lightning flashed, and thunder boomed.

Mrs. Lawrence had to see the look of concern in my eyes. "Ever hear of an umbrella?" she said. "Let Star see me shuffling down the street in the rain. At least I won't have to stand in it if she doesn't open the door. As I recall, her porch is covered."

"I'll be here," I said. "And I'll bring my dad's big golfing umbrella."

By the time I got home, Steve Sakay had called. I called him right back.

"You wanna bring the note to the store or just meet me at the corner?" he asked.

"I'll meet you at the corner," I said, "but I'll be coming around from the other way so she doesn't see me."

"This isn't some kind of a prank on her, is it?" he asked. "Because if it is, I don't want to have anything to do with—"

"Steve! I wouldn't do that! At least not anymore. The note is from an old friend of hers. It's all right. You can trust me. Does she know you're making a delivery?"

"Yeah. She was puzzled but didn't ask any questions. I just asked her if I could make my Monday delivery today."

When I met him at the corner, I asked if any of the delivery had to be put away immediately. I'd have hated to see her miss the note just because she didn't really need to do anything with the groceries.

"Oh, sure. There are perishables in there—stuff that has to be refrigerated."

"Good."

I handed him the note, and he carried the box to her porch while I watched from down the street. He slid it up to the door, rang once, knocked once, and hollered out, "Groceries!" And then he was gone. Time would tell whether Mrs. Lawrence's note would make her welcome at Mrs. Butchbaker's house.

The afternoon seemed to drag. I dropped in on Mrs.

Lawrence once just to see if she was still up to it. She was walking around the living room with her walker.

"I'll be reading some more of that stuff you brought me," she said. "I want to be prepared."

"You sure you don't want my mother to drive you? It looks like it's going to rain again."

"A little rain never hurt anybody, Tobin. Or are you afraid of it?"

"Not me."

"See you then."

The rest of the guys were jealous and said so.

"I'm still afraid of Mrs. Butchbaker," Joel said. "But I'll never call her a witch again or play tricks on her. I just wish I was going with you. Not to say anything—just to listen."

"Toby's already promised to tell us everything," Tom said. "Haven't you, Toby?"

I arrived at Mrs. Lawrence's a little early. It was a good thing. She was ready to roll. She had a shawl and rain hat on—it was raining again. My umbrella was huge with black and yellow sections that made her chuckle.

"I'm nervous," she said. "Let's get on with this. Carry my cane and my walker to the bottom of the steps, then let me lean on you with my right hand while I put my left on the rail."

She was bigger and heavier than I imagined, still we made it down the stairs all right. We were less than a block from Mrs. Butchbaker's house, but I could see already it was going to take a while to get there.

I carried the cane and didn't know how to help her with the walker, and I soon realized she didn't need any help. The rain was steady and grew heavier as we walked, so that we could hardly see in front of us.

"Just watch for high cracks in the sidewalk," she said. "The walker will roll over most of them, but if it sticks and I go down, I doubt you'll be able to get me up."

"Don't go down," I said.

"I don't plan to."

We moved slowly down the street in the rain. My heart was pounding, partly from fear that we were working Mrs. Lawrence too hard and partly from the excitement of maybe, just maybe, sitting in the same room and actually talking to Mrs. Butchbaker.

Would Pamela be there too? We wouldn't know until we got there, and we might not know then. It all depended on whether Mrs. Butchbaker let us in and admitted anything.

We finally got to the sidewalk leading back to the Butchbaker mansion. At the porch I helped Mrs. Lawrence up the stairs, putting the walker in front of her. She reached for the cane and somehow managed to carry it while working the walker too. She rang the doorbell.

I watched the windows for any sign of movement. Nothing.

She knocked once. Still nothing. Finally Mrs. Lawrence leaned forward on her walker and rapped loudly on the door several times with her cane.

"There's my one ring and my two knocks, Star!" she shouted. "And you know me well enough from half a century ago to know I'm going to stand out here until you let me in. I know you saw me coming down the street, and however stubborn you are, I'm twice as stubborn. Now I'm going to give you a minute to get to the door, and then I'm going to just stand here with my arthritis and my rheumatism and my old age until you're ashamed enough to open this door!"

I fought not to laugh, but I was also praying that Mrs. Butchbaker would open the door. I wondered what DeWayne would think or say or do to me if he saw his ancient mother, who hadn't been out of the house herself except to go to the doctor once in the last year, standing in the rain in the middle of one of my shenanigans.

I was about to suggest that Mrs. Lawrence might want to

ease herself down onto the steps to relax. That would put her back in the rain, but I could stand over her with the umbrella. The trouble was, how would I lift her to her feet when she was ready to rise?

But then I heard the door. First the lock, then the latch, then the knob. The door broke free and opened inward, but all I could see was Mrs. Butchbaker walking away.

Mrs. Lawrence turned and faced me. "I'm taking that as an invitation," she said. "You might as well too. Get on in here."

I left the umbrella leaning against the door. Mrs. Lawrence was trying to open the screen and keep her walker out of the way. "Let me do that," I said.

I sneaked a peek inside, and Mrs. Butchbaker was out of sight.

"We'll find her," Mrs. Lawrence said. "She can't get far."

Once inside, I took Mrs. Lawrence's shawl and her rain hat and put them in the corner of the entryway with her cane.

She moved down the hallway on her walker. "Where are you, Star? Don't make me play hide and seek now!"

We took a right into the parlor that I had seen when the junior deputies were pressed up against the windowpane. The shade was up now, and I could see the rain beating on the window. Mrs. Butchbaker sat in the middle of an old couch on the far side of the room. An empty coffee table sat in front of it, and two easy chairs faced the couch.

Mrs. Butchbaker sat there scowling, as if she had been defeated. Her hands were folded in her lap, and she looked exhausted. She had hidden herself from the rest of the world for fifty years, and now this old acquaintance had called her bluff and forced her way in. She glared at Mrs. Lawrence as if to ask her what she wanted.

Victoria Lawrence spoke directly. "I'm going to get right to the point, Star," she said. "I know you don't want to talk, and you don't have to. But I'm going to tell you a thing or two, and I know you can still understand English. There are people on this block who care about you and whom you have not been able to scare off with your personality. I'm one of them. We know all about you and what happened to you and your family. We know your father was a Nazi who left Germany before the worst of it, but who didn't do anything to stop the killing either.

"We know your father felt guilty when vandals burned your house and killed your little sister. We know that's why he took his own life. This boy here, Tobin Andrews, is a junior deputy. His dad's a deputy sheriff, and these boys help out all they can. They heard all the stories about you being a witch and a murderer and all that, but they cared enough to start asking questions.

"I know you married the wrong man, that he was no good and didn't treat you right, and that you had to raise your daughter by yourself. I know all about the tricks people have played on you all these years and the way you lost your mother and your siblings and your husband one by one. I know it's only you and Pamela now, Star."

For the first time, Mrs. Butchbaker moved. She flinched when Mrs. Lawrence mentioned Pamela.

"I don't know if you want to talk to me or not, Star. I can't blame you for thinking the whole world was against you. And with all the tragedy and disappointment in your life, you must have thought you were in this thing alone. You can go on being that way if you want, but I just want you to know I still care about you after all these years, and other people— even many who don't know you—care too."

Mrs. Lawrence fell silent.

I sat forward and took a breath, as if I were going to say something, but I sensed from Mrs. Lawrence that she wanted me to keep quiet.

Mrs. Butchbaker, in all her bitterness and fear, stared at

her old friend. Finally she spoke in a gravelly whisper, but in German.

"Don't start that with me now, Star," Mrs. Lawrence said. "You have to speak English to me."

Mrs. Butchbaker glared some more, crossing her arms. "You know why my father killed himself?" she managed in an accent so thick I could barely understand.

"I think I do, yes," Mrs. Lawrence said. "It is not your fault, any of it."

"I don't think you know," Mrs. Butchbaker said.

"Then tell me. If it wasn't because your sister died in the fire vandals started because your father had been a Nazi, then tell me."

Mrs. Butchbaker struggled to her feet and walked to the window. Suddenly she turned and stared at me. "You!" she said, pointing. "You were one of the young ruffians at my window, weren't you?"

"Yes, ma'am, I was," I croaked, "but we're not ruffians. We're just curious kids and—"

"And you had a taxi and a pizza man bother me in the night?"

"We feel awful about that, ma'am, and—"

"Oh, for Pete's sake!" Mrs. Lawrence said. "You're no better than the rest, Tobin!"

"I know, but we want to make it up to her, to help her, to do work for her, to help her with her daughter."

Mrs. Butchbaker nearly jumped when I mentioned her daughter. "What do *you* know about Pamela?" she demanded.

"I know she's here!" I blurted.

"How do you know that?"

"I'm guessing. What's wrong with her? Do you have to take care of her all by yourself? Can't you use some help?"

Mrs. Butchbaker began to weep, great sobs racking her body as she came back to the couch and sat again. "Pamela has a disease that should have killed her long ago," she said.

"Cystic fibrosis. She can't walk, can hardly talk. Has seen no one for years. I take care of her all day, all night."

"I'm so sorry," I said. "But there are people who would help you . . ."

"People who would help me? People only want to play tricks on me, tell stories about me. Call me a Nazi, a witch, a murderer. I know. I have ears."

"Not me and not my friends," I said. "You should give us a chance to prove it. We'll even find you help for your daughter."

Mrs. Butchbaker sat shaking her head, crying softly now.

Mrs. Lawrence leaned forward. "Star, do you want to tell me something about your father?"

The old woman, who didn't look so ugly now—just sad—nodded. "He set fire to this place himself. He could not live with the guilt."

"What guilt? The guilt of not trying to stop Hitler?"

"It was worse than that. He sold to the National Socialist Party the lumber used to build the barracks for the camps. That's what he could not live with. That's what made him so miserable."

"But surely he didn't mean to kill his own child," Mrs. Lawrence said.

"No! He didn't mean to! But he did, didn't he? God help me, I'm glad he's gone. But I still miss my sister."

Mrs. Lawrence motioned to me that I should help her stand. She moved slowly across the room with her walker, turned, and sat heavily next to her old friend. "Star," she said, embracing her, "it's time for you to let people back into your life. No more name-calling, no more tricks, no more stories. We want to know you, to talk to you, to help you. You can't bear your father's guilt any longer. That's all in the past. Will you let us love you?"

Mrs. Butchbaker sat there with her face in her hands, tears streaming down her cheeks. Mrs. Lawrence just held her and rocked her and talked softly to her. Finally, Mrs. Butchbaker reached up and hugged Mrs. Lawrence, and I thought I saw the hint of a sad smile on her face.

"Tobin," Mrs. Lawrence said, "when this rain clears up, I want you and your junior deputies down here working on this yard. Star and I are going to be busy with Pamela anyway, aren't we, Star? Now introduce me to that child again. I haven't seen her for years."

I stood when the women stood, and I was still standing there when the old woman we thought might be a witch led her aging friend, Queenie, Victoria Lawrence, down the hall to a back bedroom.

I couldn't wait to tell the junior deputies what had gone on in that house. We were going to have plenty of opportunities to prove we meant what we said. We cared.